ENGAGED TO THE BOSS

A BILLIONAIRE FAKE MARRIAGE ROMANCE

NIKKI BLOOM

This is a work of fiction. Names, characters, businesses, places, events, and incidents are fictitious products of the author's imagination. Any resemblance to actual persons, places, or events is purely coincidental.

1

POPPY

"Another, please. These things are pretty good." I made my way to the rolling bar hoping to find another mimosa with my name on it, but my fellow bridesmaids only looked at me with frowns on their faces.

"Sorry, babe, it's all gone." Stephine was the one to dish out the bad news.

"Seriously?" I pushed past her and stared at the empty platter. "But how? There were a ton of them just a second ago. We couldn't have drunk through them already, or else there's someone here who's about to join Alcoholics Anonymous."

"That would be the bride," answered Beth, another member of the wedding party – the maid of honor. Jenna and I were good friends but Beth was practically Jenna's sister. Besides, Beth was better at all the girly wedding stuff anyway. Just looking at the corset on the back of Jenna's dress had given me a headache. You'd think it'd be pretty straightforward, like lacing up a shoe or something but trust me, it was a thousand times harder than that.

"Guys, am I making the right decision here?" Jenna

came bustling into the room wearing nothing but her dressing robe. Her hair, however, was still looking pretty spectacular, if I do say so myself. I had given her a romantic bun that hugged the nap of her neck. A few curls framed the shape of her face, softening her expression to an almost angelic state. I had never seen her look so beautiful. She was *glowing*.

I guess that's what happens when a girl gets married. I could only hope that the same would apply to me on the day of my wedding...

If that day ever happened to roll around, that is.

"Oh, honey." Beth came up behind her and rubbed both her shoulders. "You love Hudson, don't you?"

"Of course, I do!" she exclaimed. "I do!"

"Then, what are you worried about?"

"I just can't help but think... What if something happens? What if we go our separate ways? Divorces are never pretty..."

I took a seat by the fireplace, right across from the bride. She was an outdoorsy sort of person and as a result, her skin was always blessed with that golden hue other girls would die for. But at this moment, she was looking a little pale, maybe even a tad green around the edges. "Chill," I said, leaning forward to place my hand on her knee. "You've been planning this wedding for the last two years, counting down the days. To be honest, when you first started dating that lumberjack, I didn't think things would work out in the long term, but it has and there's no arguing that the big ol' lug makes you happy. That's all that matters, isn't it?"

A member of the hotel waitstaff entered the room with a tray of fresh mimosas.

Jenna jumped out of her seat and lunged towards the

alcohol. It was no easy feat but somehow, I managed to grab her by the waist and hold her back.

"Let. Go. Of. Me." Jenna sounded like some sort of rabid animal, ready to bite my face clean off my skull.

"You don't want to show up at your wedding drunk, do you?"

"All I want right now is to take the edge off."

"How about you start with breathing?" I forced her onto the couch. The other bridesmaids backed me up, standing around the bride so she couldn't do anything stupid. "Look, I know you must be nervous, but this isn't anything but cold feet. Once you start down the aisle and see your husband-to-be standing at the altar, you'll come to realize that you were right to marry the guy."

"And what if that doesn't happen?"

BY SOME MIRACLE, we got Jenna into her dress. But that was only half the battle.

"Suck it in!" I shouted as I tugged on the built-in corset. No one told me about this step, or the fact there were about a million eye-and-hooks that needed to be done up in order to give Jenna the hourglass figure she was hoping for. "I said...suck...it...in..."

"If I suck in any harder, I won't be able to breathe!"

"I don't care about that. You were the one who bought a dress with this infernal contraption so now you are going to face the consequences of your decisions." I had one foot on the wall for leverage. I was going to get Jenna into the corset even if it killed us both.

"Uh...Poppy? Maybe you should ease up a bit..."

"Quiet!" I snapped. At this point, I was sweating

bullets. Jenna, too. I clenched my teeth and tugged, managing to get a few more hooks into place. I was so close to the finish line now. All I needed now were a few more tugs...

Snap!

And there went the seam...

I threw up my hands in defeat.

In the end, Jenna decided to go on without it. Thank the fucking stars.

And Beth, the genius, figured out how to do the laces up the back. Finally, we were cooking with fire. Note to self – keep the wedding dress simple. These ballgowns are more work than their worth.

"But they are incredibly beautiful. You have to admit that Jenna looks like some sort of princess," came a voice at the back of my voice and it was true. Jenna was *radiant*. I could not deny it. Seeing her sparked a jealousy deep inside of me. She was about to marry the love of her life while I was still a resident of Singleville and it sucked. I could do without the relationship drama, sure, but it got kind of lonely at night, you know? Having a bed all to yourself becomes kind of a bummer after a while.

It was time for me to change that.

And Jenna's wedding was the perfect place to start. She had assured me that there would be plenty of available bachelors and I was keen to believe her.

Beth had tried to talk me out of it – that it would be tasteless of me. I had no intention of listening to her. She was much too proper – always a Goodie Two-Shoes. Sometimes, a girl just needs to let loose and have a bit of fun. I wasn't planning on hurting anyone, so why did it matter what I did behind closed doors?

"Poppy?" I looked up and saw Jenna standing there

looking like a bridezilla. For a second, I saw my life flash before my eyes.

"It's time to go. If you make me late for my wedding, I'm going to kill you."

"Sorry," I said as I got up and quickly finished off the rest of my mimosa. The warmth of the room had rendered it lukewarm and disgusting. The bitter taste lingered in my mouth. I had half a mind to gargle some mouthwash, but if I lingered another moment, I was more than certain that Jenna would serve my head on a silver platter to all of her guests. It wouldn't make a very good obituary. So, thinking I would avoid the casualty, I sucked it up and followed the bridal party down to the elevator.

"What were you daydreaming about, anyway?" asked Jenna as she nervously twirled her bouquet. Some of the petals were too fragile to handle the velocity. With a gentle grace, they fluttered to the floor.

"How I am going to get laid tonight."

She rolled her eyes. "You can't be serious."

"I am."

"At *my* wedding?"

"Where else? You were the one who told me about all the cute bachelors on your guest list."

"I didn't think you were going to hunt them down for a one-night stand."

I answered her with a shrug. "It's not every day that I get to come out and enjoy Hawaii's sandy beaches. I might as well make the most of this little slice of paradise." I ended with a playful wink which was meant to ease things up a bit, but Jenna didn't look very happy with me. I'm just going to blame it on the pre-marriage jitters. Normal Jenna would be cheering me on. She was always trying to hook me up with someone or the other.

Ding!

The elevator doors slid open and we filed out, one by one. From there, we ducked into the limo and made our way to the wedding site – a beautiful beach with miles of sand and a backdrop of crystal-clear ocean.

It's when we got there that things really started to get interesting.

2

CONNOR

"Wait, what do you mean he got sick with the flu? Tell him to take a shit-ton of Nyquil and get his ass over here!"

I stood in the doorway.

The bride-to-be looked like she was about to explode but then again, Jenna had a habit of doing that. She might have been my half-sister, but we hadn't grown up together. Even so, I knew her well enough to recognize the scathing anger growing on her face. If she didn't calm down, there would be hell to pay and I certainly didn't want to get in the middle of it.

"That won't be necessary," I said.

The suddenness of my appearance was enough to get everyone to quiet down. I was just about to explain myself when I felt the weight of someone's gaze, heavier than all the rest.

She was sitting across the room, one leg crossed over the other, a crystal glass between her fingers. Now, I am no stranger to beautiful women. I tend to be a kind of magnet, attracting them far and wide. I'd like to say that they're quick to fall for my devilish charm but that's not it at all. It's the money – always the money. They want the diamond rings and the fancy vacations to exotic parts of the world. They dream of the glitz and the glamor thinking it will make them happy, but they don't know the truth.

But this girl was staring at me with a curious sheen in her eyes and her stare lingered, too, unlike all the other bridesmaids.

"Connor?" Jenna reeled around to face me with her eyes wide like she had never seen me before. "What the hell are you doing here? I thought you said that you wouldn't be able to make it because of some important business meeting." She paused, looking me once over. "And is that Gabriele's suit?"

"It is," I confirmed. "Your fiancé gave me a call last night to tell me that his best man had fallen sick with the flu and that he's bedridden at the moment."

"Aaron called you?"

"Last I checked, I was speaking English here."

Jenna growled loud enough for me to take a step back. "I'm not here to play games with you."

"Alright, alright," I said, holding up both my hands in a display of innocence. "Long story short, I'm taking the place of your fiancé's best man because, evidently, we're the same suit size."

Her eyes widened further. I was starting to worry that they would pop right out of her head and that wouldn't be very becoming of a soon-to-be bride.

"I could kiss you!" She wrapped her arms around my neck and hugged me so tightly that it became quite difficult to breathe.

"What's stopping you?"

She glared. If looks could kill, yeah, I'd be in a casket already.

With the crisis averted, Jenna went on to freak out about something else. I wasn't surprised. She was always getting herself riled up. How her fiancé managed to deal with her on a daily basis was beyond my measure of understanding. And yet, in the times that I had seen them together, they seemed nothing but happy. The way they looked at each other said everything that needed to be said – they loved each other.

I was still waiting for someone to give me that special look of adoration, but I was starting to think that maybe the girl of my dreams was just that – a dream. She didn't really exist, and I was just a fool wasting my time trying to find her.

"Hey, Connor, was it? Looks like you're stuck with me." It was the girl with the green eyes – the same one who had looked at me with such intensity.

"My bouquet! Has anyone seen my bouquet?" Bridezilla was at it again. She was tearing apart the place looking for the flowers. I swear, marriage does something to women on a mental level. Of all the weddings I had ever been to, I don't think I've seen a bride not in some level of freak out mode.

"How long until she notices?" the green-eyed girl whispered in my direction.

"Hmm?" I looked up and saw that she was holding two bouquets. One was much smaller than the other and the stems were wrapped in a ribbon of deep burgundy. The other looked like it had been dipped in liquid glitter. "May I?"

She handed it over. "These don't even smell like real flowers."

"That's because they blast them with hairspray so that they last longer."

"Hairspray?" I questioned. "You're pulling my leg."

"If you say so." For some reason, the grin on her face had stretched from ear to ear. Her gaze was no longer on my face but aimed directly behind me. Wondering what it was that she was seeing, I turned around, but it was too late.

Wham!

"Think this is funny, do you?" wailed the bride as I stumbled backward, holding the back of my head. She snatched the bouquet from my hands and stormed off. I could just about see the steam billowing from her ears. Oh, how I pitied the groom.

Lingering by the refreshment table, the green-eyed woman still wore that grin on her face. I was starting to get the sense that she was the mischievous type. I kind of liked it.

"You set me up for that," I said, helping myself to a glass of champagne.

"Did I?" came her innocent response. "Although, if I remember correctly, *you* were the one who wanted to see the bouquet. As far as I'm concerned, you brought Jenna's wrath upon yourself." She popped a mint into her mouth before sitting down and crossing one leg over the other. The slit of her dress caused the fabric to fall to either side, exposing the silky skin of her upper thigh.

"That's the cue! That's the cue!" cried the bride. She started pushing people out of the room. It was chaos. Everyone got jumbled together. One bridesmaid tripped over the hem of her dress causing a domino effect. The groomsmen were dragged forward by their partners because they clearly had no idea what they were supposed to be doing. My green-eyed vixen, however, was nowhere to be seen. I scanned the crowd trying to find her but just then, I felt my phone start to vibrate with an incoming call.

It wasn't the best time for me to answer, but when I saw my lawyer's number flashing across the screen, I knew that I had to take it. I broke off from the group and stood underneath the shade of a nearby umbrella. The seaside wind was blowing into the phone's receiver, making it impossible to hear what my lawyer was saying. "Dan, I'm going to need you to say that again!" Shouting was my only option.

"Keep shouting like that and Jenna is going to have your balls on a chopping block." The green-eyed beauty reappeared just as quickly as she had disappeared. Her warning was a whisper but I heard it loud and clear. "And that would be a crying shame." She grabbed my arm and pulled on it to get me to move. "Stand to my right. You really don't want to give Jenna any reason to single you out from the herd. Getting married has deranged her a bit. Take my advice and stay on her good side."

I dropped my phone into my pocket, choosing to ignore it even as it vibrated. It wasn't every day that I allowed a call to go to voicemail, but I wanted to hear what this girl had to say – to hear the silkiness of her voice and have it wrap around my head. "I'm surprised."

"Are you?"

"You had little regard for my wellbeing when you handed over Jenna's bouquet."

"Maybe I feel guilty and I'm trying to make amends for the pain and suffering I may have caused you. Or..." she leaned forward, the words hanging on her lips. "...maybe I want to keep you alive long enough to know your name."

"Connor," I said. "Yours?"

"Pomona but everyone calls me Poppy."

"Well, you have my dearest apologies, Poppy. It was

terribly rude of me not to introduce myself. Will you ever find it in your heart to forgive me?"

She tried to keep a straight face but I could see the beginnings of a grin on her lips. "It depends."

"On?"

"Tell me one thing, and there is only one right answer to this question."

"You're setting the stakes pretty high, but I think I'm up to the challenge. What's the question?"

"Are you a dog person or a cat person?"

I considered her for a moment. She could really swing either way. I could imagine her with some glasses on, reading a good book, and curled up with a feline friend. But, at the same time, I could see her on a hiking trail with a four-legged companion following in her midst. "To be honest, I never had any pets while growing up. My grand-parents were the ones who raised me and they did a lot of traveling, so it just wasn't practical for us to have a family pet. Although, if I was hard-pressed to choose, I'd pick a dog over a cat. I like to keep myself active and it would be nice to have a running partner."

"What kind of breed?" she asked like it would make or break her opinion of me.

"Uh...rescue?"

She laughed. It was a mirthful sound that brought an immediate smile to my face. "That was clever of you. Rescuing a dog is very noble, so my only question now is why haven't you gotten yourself a dog?"

"Do you work for a rescue organization or something?" I asked. "I didn't think I would get hounded into adopting a dog when I agreed to attend this wedding."

"I'm just trying to make conversation," she said. "We've been standing around all morning. The constant flow of mimosas has really been the only thing keeping me sane. All these girls want to talk about is the latest model of shapewear or how their kids have learned to go to the bathroom. I'm hoping you might prove to be a bit more interesting, so tell me something about yourself. I mean, you might think we're close to the finish line but Jenna will probably bitch about something and that'll push the start of the ceremony another half hour – maybe an hour if we're really unfortunate. I haven't even danced and already my feet are killing me. I should have listened to myself and gotten a pair of fancy flip flops."

"Why didn't you?"

She showed me her footwear. "Because these were on sale and I couldn't resist a bargain. I'm a typical woman in that sense."

"Ah. Well, we can always trade."

"Trade?" She took one look at my feet and doubled over. "We would both like clowns. You must be double my size. I'm not even sure if you could get your pinky toe into my heels, let alone your entire foot."

"Then just ditch the shoes."

"I already told you, I got them for a bargain. I can't let them go."

"You know, I will never understand a woman's obsession with shoes. They are just shoes."

"Would the two of you quiet down? They're going to hear you." Another member of the wedding party shushed us. I hadn't realized we were laughing so hard. She gestured toward a field of chairs, each one of them filled with family and friends. A few of them were looking our way, waiting for us to do something.

And we did. Once the first couple started moving, we all did. It was quite difficult to walk through the sand, but I had it easy compared to the girls wearing high heels. All I can say is that it wasn't very graceful. But somehow, we all made it to the arch where the bride and groom were to get married. There, each couple separated – bridesmaids to the left, groomsmen to the right. Once the front row was filled, the music changed.

Everyone turned in their seats. And there came the bride marching toward the beach. She had this bright smile on her face, eyes focused on her husband-to-be. It was like nothing else mattered to her.

Buzz. Buzz.

My hand immediately went into my pocket. I was just about to pull out my phone when I felt a burning stare in my peripheral vision. I turned in that direction to find my green-eyed partner looking my way. It would be terribly rude of me to answer the call in the middle of a wedding and I didn't want Poppy to think I was some kind of scumbag. There was still the rest of the night to be had and I wanted her to feel comfortable spending it with me. So, whoever was calling would just have to wait.

I tried to focus on the ceremony, but the officiant was awfully dull and that's saying a lot from someone like me. In my line of work, being stuck in a conference room full of boring old men is an almost daily occurrence. But this guy had a monotoned voice and an excitement level of negative hundred. There was absolutely no emotion on any part of his face. It made staying awake an almost Herculean task. And I wasn't the only one struggling. I could see slouching bodies, drooping heads, and heavy eyelids.

But there was one person who seemed oddly alert. Only, she wasn't watching the exchange between the bride and groom. She was watching *me*. Those dazzling green eyes of hers kept darting in my direction, half-hidden by the curtain of red hair framing her face. I couldn't quite be sure but it looked like she was smiling – the kind of smile worn by someone who knows something they shouldn't. What was she thinking? What game was she playing?

She became my sole focus for the rest of the ceremony because everyone else seemed to pale in comparison. What was it about this woman? Why did she have this hold over me? Why did I want to know everything about her? From her favorite dessert to how she took her coffee – whether she even liked coffee. I wanted to find myself locked in a room with her just to talk the night away.

"I now pronounce you husband and wife. You may kiss the bride."

3

POPPY

Starving, I made my getaway. Jenna and her new husband would be busy for the next couple of hours taking pictures. The bridal party was supposed to meet back up with them around two. Until then, I was free to do whatever I wanted, and this girl can't survive on water-downed mimosas alone.

So, I hiked up my skirt and made my way towards the boardwalk. It was packed with tourists. A few of them stared as I walked by. Jenna hadn't picked the most flattering color scheme. Any brighter and my dress would have been mistaken for a highlighter. But try telling that to Jenna.

My thoughts were interrupted by the smell of a pizzeria. I could pick out all the different aromas from bubbling cheese to the sizzling of crisp pepperoni. Best of all was the scent of garlic bread. Maybe this was one of those places with the fancy crust. Eager to find out, I turned into the shop. The dining room was tiny and the woman behind the counter looked surprised to see me like she had never spotted a living customer before.

"Where are your manners, Genevieve?" came the voice

of an older man. He had materialized from the kitchen wearing an apron covered in flour. "Get the lass a menu. She didn't come in here to gawk at the décor."

The woman grabbed one of the takeout menus and hurried to my table. "Can I get you anything to drink?"

"A water is fine," I said. "I don't mean to be rude by asking this, but do you guys not get a lot of customers or something?" A quick look through the window was enough to tell me that most of the other restaurants were packed with people. What made this place so different? Was there something I was missing? Had someone completely trashed the pizzeria online or something?

"We do most of our business through delivery," she explained. "To the university nearby. Most of the tourists want something more than a pizzeria."

"Ah," I said with a nod. "So, why are you paying for this space on the boardwalk? I mean, rent has to be outrageous and it doesn't really make much sense to be paying an arm and a leg if you don't get the foot traffic the boardwalk is supposed to bring."

"Very well said." It was a familiar voice.

Connor.

He stood in the doorway of the pizzeria. Had he followed me here?

"Sounds to me like someone studied business in college."

"It wasn't my major, but I did take a few classes."

"It shows."

Genevieve now stood with bulging eyes. It appeared that two living, breathing customers sitting in her dining room was too much for her to take. The old man from the kitchen had to tow her away.

"I've been meaning to ask you something."

"And what might that be?" I asked in a casual tone while browsing the menu. Everything on it sounded exceptionally good. Either that or I was just really hungry and willing to eat just about anything. "What are your thoughts on buffalo chicken pizza?"

"There has to be bleu cheese on the side."

"Definitely," I agreed. "Now, what was it that you wanted to ask me?"

"If you could spend the next year of your life doing whatever you wanted, what would it be and why?"

"That's what you wanted to ask me?"

"Well, you said you wanted to get to know me. The feeling is mutual. I thought this would be a good question to get the ball rolling. Although, I'll admit, I didn't come up with it on my own. Some blogger suggested it along with ten other questions. Apparently, if we go through all ten we'll figure out whether or not we're soulmates."

"Right," I said with a chuckle. "And my horoscope is going to predict exactly what's going to happen to me."

"Speaking of horoscopes, what's your sign? I can see whether we're compatible."

"Damn, you're persistent. I'll give you that." I smiled over the rim of my drink before taking a sip. "Sagittarius," I said. "You?"

"Aries."

"Shame. We're both fire signs. You know what that means? We're bound to butt heads."

"I wouldn't be surprised. I've been known to be stubborn."

"That's the ram in you," I said. "I've known a few Aries in my lifetime and they can be pretty difficult to deal with. But I'll admit you're rubbing me the right way. You definitely beat the original best man. That guy is a bore and a half and he likes to nag, too. You? You're okay – for now. We'll see how I feel about you at the end of the night."

Before Connor could respond, the old man approached our table. "Have you two decided what you'll be having?"

"We'll be sharing a large buffalo chicken pizza. Bleu cheese on the size. And an order of the mozzarella sticks. Oh, and an order of fries, too." Before I could order anything else, I returned the menu. I was hungry, sure, but I wanted my dress to continue to fit me when I went back for pictures.

"That's quite the appetite."

I shrugged. "What can I say? I like to eat."

"There's nothing wrong with that. I can't stand the girls who go to a restaurant and order nothing but a plain salad, and then I have to sit there and watch them grimace the entire time."

"Sounds like you run into that problem quite often."

"Don't get the wrong idea. It's not like I'm taking out women on dates every other day. Besides, most of the time, this happens at business meetings."

"Oh, I'm sure," I said before taking a sip from my water. I mean, this guy was devilishly handsome – handsome enough to be on the cover of a magazine. With looks like that, I wouldn't have been surprised to find women lining up at his doorstep. And with a personality like his, he could have the cream of the crop. There was a good chance he was already taken – that he had swept some girl off her feet with that charming smile of his. "In any case, why did you follow me here?"

"What makes you think that I followed you?"

"I have eyes, you know. That watch you're wearing – it didn't come from a department store, did it?" I grabbed his hand and brought it across the table so I could take a better look at the timepiece on his wrist. Just as I had guessed – a Rolex – and it looked real too, not one of those cheap knock-offs that people wear to make themselves appear wealthier than they were. Honestly, I didn't understand the obsession with brand names. A $30 watch told time just as well as a $3,000 watch.

"Hmm?"

Now that the bad boy was out in the open, the watch glittered like mad. "I bet this thing is worth more money than the typical mortgage."

"Well, aren't you the observant one."

For some reason, I kept holding on to his hand. Doing so brought a tingling sensation to my skin and I liked it a bit too much to want it to stop.

My core temperature rose. I could feel the blood rushing to my cheeks. Quickly, I took another sip of water, wanting to cool myself down, but then I made the mistake of looking into his eyes. That's when my insides began to boil but in the best possible way. "You still haven't answered my question," I said, trying to play it cool even though my whole face was turning into a giant McIntosh apple.

"Isn't it obvious?" he answered.

"Actually, no."

"Well, I'm sure you'll figure it out."

"And if I don't?"

"Then I guess you'll never know." The legs of his chair scraped against the ground as he positioned himself closer. "But I'll give you a hint. Caviar isn't worth the price."

My eyebrows furrowed together. "What does that have to do with anything?"

He just smiled. When his words failed to spark under-standing, he occupied himself by folding a napkin.

"Caviar...?" I questioned but he ignored me, focusing instead on his origami project.

A paper crane appeared in the palm of his hand. He pulled on the tail, causing the wings to flap. As he did so, the old man returned with our pizza while Genevieve carried over the sides.

The crust was nice and golden with baked-in parmesan. The cheese heaped over the buffalo chicken bubbled. And the smell? Like a Super Bowl party concentrated into a 16-inch circumference.

"Enjoy," said the old man. "And Genevieve will be sure to bring out some extra water. The buffalo can be quite spicy."

"Nothing I can't handle," boasted Conner.

Then, it came to me. "Wait, are you telling me that a rich boy like you actually prefers cheap pizzeria food?"

He answered by dunking his slice into the bleu cheese dressing and taking a bite. A second later, he spat it back onto his plate while fanning his mouth.

"Too spicy for you?"

"No. Hot." He spoke like someone struggling with a cheek full of marbles.

"I could have told you that. See this?" I pointed to the steam rolling off the surface. "That means that it's hot."

He stopped.

"You know, if looks could kill, I'd be on my way to the morgue right about now," I said, doing my best to suppress a giggle. Having lunch with Connor made me feel like I was back in high school, going out on a first date. Back then, if a guy asked you out, it was a big deal and an even bigger deal for me who wore braces for my entire teenage years.

There was a moment of silence before we both fell into

a fit of laughter. By the time I managed to catch my breath, my stomach was hurting me. "You know, I think I like you."

"Is that so?" It was then that his phone began to vibrate. He watched it skid across the table for no longer than a millisecond before snatching it up. "Bill. I've been waiting for your call all day. Did you get those numbers?" He had gotten out of his seat. Forgetting all about our meal, he began to pace the entire length of the restaurant. "What do you mean you need more time? I've given you an extension already. I'm not dicking around here. I *need* those numbers and if you can't find them for me, I'll have to find someone who can. Do I make myself clear?"

It was like a switch had been flipped. One second we were enjoying some pizza and a couple of laughs and the next, he was threatening to fire some poor bloke.

No longer hungry, I beckoned Genevieve to the table. "A check and a to-go box, please."

WHEN NEXT I SAW CONNOR, he was still on his phone. It was like he had surgically attached it to his ear. I could understand taking a business call but there was a time and place and this certainly wasn't it. Out of the corner of my eye, I spotted Jenna. If she noticed Connor yammering on his phone, I feared the repercussions. Becoming a Mrs. hadn't toned down her bridezilla levels.

Wanting to warn him, I walked over and grabbed his wrist. "Hey, you might want to hang up," I said. "Jenna's coming.

"Just give me a minute," he mouthed, hand over the receiver.

"You don't have a minute. Jenna wants pictures and if

you're caught posing with that phone, she's going to stuff it so far up your ass that it'll come out your mouth." I was speaking loud enough so that whomever was on the line could hear me.

"Sorry, Derrek...I've got to go."

"Now, come on. Let's get this over with. I've never been a fan of pictures. I always look so awkward and my smile is absolute shit. My parents paid so much money to get my teeth straightened out and I keep them hidden."

"I don't know why." He stopped to look at me, his eyes soft like he was admiring something precious. "I think you have a beautiful smile and an even more beautiful laugh. If you want I can crack some jokes during the photoshoot."

"What makes you think I'll laugh?"

"Because they are comedic gold," he answered. "And if I fail to make you laugh, well, I'll take you out to dinner or something to make up for it. How does that sound?"

"Are you asking me out on a date?" I asked.

He did not answer me outright but there was a mischievous grin stretching across his lips as we crossed the lawn, joining the rest of the bridal party that was already there.

"Where have you been?" Jenna wheeled on us the second she saw our approach. "I was about ready—"

"We're here now, aren't we? That's all that matters, isn't it?" I interrupted, thinking it would be the best way to stop her from blowing up.

From there, the photographer took over. He took about a million pictures. There were some of us jumping in the air and some of us all together, smiling with the sea against our backs.

With every picture, it was a new joke. Some of them were actually pretty good and I have to admit, I was rather surprised. I didn't think Connor was the kind of guy to crack jokes. From the watch that he wore to the obsession with his phone, I thought him nothing more than a businessman, but it appeared that Connor had a few tricks hidden up his sleeve and a few good punchlines, too.

"Hey, did you hear about the three guys on a boat?"

"No, I didn't," I said in reply as we all posed in front of a giant oak tree. The photographer was busy getting the train of Jenna's dress into the shot. "What about them?"

"Well, these three guys had four cigarettes but they didn't have a light, so one guy thought to throw one of the cigarettes overboard and the boat became a cigarette lighter."

I laughed just as the photographer snapped the first shot. Looks like Connor had saved himself from buying me dinner.

WITH THE PICTURES OVER, we filed into the limousine. "This is quite the event," commented someone toward the front. A bottle of champagne was opened, the white foam spilling over the side.

"Do you know what comes next?" It was Connor. After the photo shoot he had answered another one of his business calls and it had left him mute to the rest of the world.

"Damn, I'm surprised that phone of yours has any battery left. You were on that call an awfully long time." To be completely honest, I was a little annoyed with his behavior. When his phone was tucked away in his pocket, I could enjoy his company. He made for good conversation and he was pretty successful at making me laugh, but whenever he took a call, I was left twiddling my thumbs and I don't particularly care for being ignored – frankly, I don't think anyone does.

"There was something of a crisis at work, but I think I have it under control," he said. "I know, you must think me a jerk or something."

"I just thought it was common for people to leave work at the office when they attend a wedding."

"I wish," he said. "But that's the curse of managing a business. It has a way of following you everywhere. Trust me, if I walked away, there's a good chance the whole operation would crash and burn."

"Let's test that theory, shall we?" I held out my hand. "Give me the phone."

"What?"

"You heard me. Earlier, you made a bet with me that you could make me laugh during the photoshoot; now I'm betting that your company can survive a couple of hours without you."

"But what if something happens and they need me?"

"They'll just have to figure it out on their own. Besides, how are you supposed to have any fun tonight if you're busy worrying about your phone? Trust me, you'll thank me for this later."

He looked hesitant, dubious even. If I had to guess, he had never been without his phone before. It probably felt like I was amputating his pinky finger or something. I didn't think he would agree to it but then I saw the nod of his head. "Fine, fine," he consented. "But you aren't going to do anything–"

Before he could finish, I slid the phone into the front part of my dress, right between the girls. He'd have to be pretty bold or pretty desperate to try and get it back from me.

"Do you think that's going to stop me?"

"Well, if you start reaching for my breasts, that gives me and the whole bridal party a reason to slap you. Is a phone call really worth the wrath of all these women?"

"I guess you got me there." He rested his now-empty hands behind his head. "Okay, so now that you've got my full attention, what do you want to talk about?"

"You asked me what was next and good thing, too, because you're going to want to listen. You never attended any of the rehearsals so I'm assuming you know nothing about the entrance dance."

"Dance?" He sat up and a bump in the road nearly caused our heads to bang together. We were saved the headache only by a couple of inches. The tips of our noses brushed together and suddenly, it felt incredibly warm inside the limo. I glanced towards the nearest window but it was too far for me to reach. Besides, it wasn't like I could move. Trapped in his gaze, I had become frozen in place, losing all train of thought.

Are his lips getting even closer? I thought as I felt the warmth of his breath.

"I'm not much of a dancer," he admitted, his voice a raspy whisper. "Only under *special* occasions and very rarely on the dancefloor."

He meant something by that, but my mind was so muddled that I couldn't make much sense of it. "Well, I don't think we have a choice."

Another bump and we were thrown back into our seats. Whatever magic had surrounded us was gone. I was left with a shiver and a sense of emptiness like someone had carved out my insides.

"Or else Jenna will have my head?"

"That's right," I confirmed.

"When I agreed to do this for her, I never expected that I'd be jumping through so many hoops. This whole thing feels like one giant circus." He grabbed a couple of bottles of purified water. He opened them both before handing one my way.

I thanked him and took a sip. My mouth was incredibly dry. I wanted to blame it on the stuffiness of the limousine, but I had a feeling that something – or rather, someone – else was to blame.

"Since we're on the topic, why did you agree to be the replacement? I have to assume that you and Jenna are pretty close if she called on you to help."

"She's my half-sister."

"What?" The water bottle slipped from my grip by a couple of inches. I managed to tighten my hold before it could spill all over my dress. "That would make you her half-brother."

"That's usually how these things work."

"But Jenna never told me anything about you!"

"I don't know why. I'm pretty awesome if I do say so myself."

"If you're so awesome, why didn't she include you in the original bridal party?"

He pointed right between my breasts. "I think it probably has to do with the fact that I'm a workaholic. As you keep reminding me, I can be pretty oblivious about knowing when it's inappropriate to take a phone call."

I didn't bother to answer. We had stopped at a red light. I took the opportunity to jump towards the front of the limousine.

"Hey!"

"Watch it!"

The light turned green and we started forward. The

momentum of it nearly took me off my feet. Someone grabbed me by the arm and steadied me from falling. "Thanks," I mumbled under my breath, not even bothering to look in their direction.

"Jenna."

The bride looked up. She opened her mouth to say something but with the limousine's next stop, I was thrust right into her lap.

"Oomph!" she groaned as she tried to pull me off of her but there was really nowhere for me to go. For such long vehicles, limousines are incredibly cramped.

"You didn't tell me that Connor was your half-brother!" I hissed, still on her lap. "We've been friends for how many years now?"

Some of the others caught wind of our conversation. It seemed like I wasn't the only one kept in the dark.

"I can't believe you never mentioned him. If I had a hot half-brother, I totally would have told you that he existed."

"Well, I just never thought the two of you would hit it off. He isn't really your type."

"Still!" I took her by the shoulders and shook her as if that might make her understand. "How could you keep this from me? He's your half-brother!"

Jenna's husband had to stop me before I could give his new bride some serious brain damage.

4

CONNOR

We arrived at the venue. It was a beautiful Victorian mansion privately rented for the occasion. White-gloved servers greeted us, holding platters of hors d'oeuvres. Many of the groomsmen flocked towards the servers only to stop in bewilderment as soon as they saw the alien concoctions spaced evenly upon the surface.

"What the hell is that stuff?" mumbled the best man.

"Escargot," answered the server.

"Isn't that...snail?" The groomsman asking the question was looking a little queasy. He stumbled backward, eyeing the escargot with suspicion like he expected it to come flying at his face at any moment.

"You know, it's actually quite good, especially if you like garlic," I said as I sidled up to Poppy. "But seeing as you ran off with our pizza, I can't see how you'd be very hungry right now."

"Hey, I paid for that pizza. As far as I'm concerned, that pizza is mine."

"If this is about who's paying for things then I think it's a good time to tell you that I'm the one fitting this entire bill." I waved my arm towards the mansion. "You see, owning your own business comes with its benefits. This place belongs to one of my clients. A doctor who owns a private practice. Charges an arm and a leg but I was able to haggle him down a bit for this place. Jenna nearly lost her mind when I told her that I had booked—"

"Really?" Poppy interrupted. I couldn't be certain but she sounded a little clipped. I would have thought her at least a little bit impressed but her face was as smooth as marble. "Jenna is lucky to have a half-brother who is so generous with his money. This really is her dream wedding." Her body language said it all. Arms crossed. Posture rigid. She hadn't stopped tapping her foot.

"Poppy!" It was one of the other bridesmaids. She came around and swept off with Poppy, leaving me to stand there. I wanted to make sense of what had just happened, but her bitterness had been so abrupt that it had taken me by surprise. Was she angry that I was paying for the wedding? But how did that make any sense? As she said herself, I was funding Jenna's dream wedding. As Jenna's friend, wouldn't she be happy that Jenna was getting exactly what she wanted?

Before I could come to a conclusion, the wedding coordinator gave a whistle that was loud enough to make every head turn. "Everyone, I want you to partner up. The guests are waiting inside, and I think they have waited long enough."

Poppy returned to my side but didn't even bother to look at me. "Was it something I said?"

"When we get inside, there's a routine we're supposed to follow—"

Buzz!

She gave a startled jump as her breasts began to vibrate.

"It's probably someone from work," I said. "If you would only let me check..." The words were out of my mouth before I even realized I had said them.

For a second, I thought she would comply with my request, but I should have known by the devilish smile on her face that she wouldn't. "I think work can wait. After all, Jenna did say that she wanted an unplugged reception. I mean, you wouldn't want to ruin her dream wedding, would you?"

"What the hell did I do to piss you off?" I asked her point-blank, hoping for an answer while knowing it would prove rather useless. Women have this way of toying with you. They like to make you figure out what you did wrong instead of just telling you what's really upsetting them.

Buzz. Buzz.

I was dying to know who was calling. It could have been anyone and for any reason. I had half a mind to grab it from her, thinking I could take her by surprise as we marched toward the reception hall. Music reverberated underfoot. The DJ was announcing the incoming party. A round of applause followed. I could no longer tell if my phone was vibrating. "Poppy, please. Just tell me what's bothering you."

The doors opened back. The maid of honor and best man stepped forward, pumping their arms into the air. When they reached the middle of the room, the song shifted to something in the tango genre. He took her by the wrist. A rose had materialized in his hand. He brought it to his mouth and stepped off the dance floor, waiting for the next couple to show off their moves.

"Wait, what are we supposed to do?"

"Maybe if you weren't so busy bragging about your money, you would have thought to ask me."

"Bragging? You think I was bragging?"

"You weren't very modest," she answered.

"Look, I'm sorry. I wasn't trying to brag, but you really can't blame me for being proud of the fact that I helped my sister out with her wedding. She was going to settle for a backyard wedding had I not stepped in."

"Up next we have Poppy and Connor!" And just like that we were out on the dance floor. Poppy had plastered a smile on her face that was so fake that she looked like a defective doll and I looked like some deranged puppet with my arms pumping into the air.

And then it happened – a shift in the music – something I actually recognized. I was worried we'd be left to dance to some electric garbage.

"Ah..." A genuine smile overtook my lips. "The mambo. This I can do."

Poppy was already walking towards the others, but she wouldn't get away from me quite so easily. I glanced first at our watching audience before leaning in her direction, arm outstretched. Our fingertips brushed together. She stopped. That's when I made my move. With one tug of her arm, she was pinned against me. We were locked together, hip to hip.

"What are you doing?"

"What does it look like I'm doing?" My hand slipped to the small of her back, dangerously close to her ass. My other hand found hers, clasping it in a tight hold. Without waiting another beat, I guided her through the footwork, letting our bodies move like water, fluid and free. "Dancing," I answered as I bent her backward, far enough for her hair to sweep the floor and her leg to rise into the air, foot nearly at my ear. "And having a hell of a time." I pulled her back into a standing position so that our faces were only inches apart.

She was breathing hard despite the fact that we hadn't been dancing for very long.

Her bottom lip shook ever so slightly. I could imagine biting into it – to taste the sweetness that was sure to be there.

"Hey now, no hogging the dance floor because next, we have the bride and groom!" The room erupted with applause as Jenna and her husband emerged, following a routine all their own.

I noticed that Poppy wasn't quite watching them. Instead, she kept smoothing out the skirt of her dress. "Is something the matter with it?" I asked.

She looked up. "Where did you learn to dance like that?"

"Why? Did you like it?"

"That isn't what I said."

"I could give you some private lessons if you'd like."

Another round of applause announced the end of their first dance. The bridal party shuffled toward the head table. Dinner would be served soon.

A whole army of servers surfaced from the woodwork, carrying the starter salad. A quiet din filled the room. I waited for Poppy to say something, but she seemed far more interested in picking out the raisins from her salad.

"What do you have against raisins?"

"Well, they sort of freak me out. They look like little bugs, especially in a salad."

I couldn't help but chuckle. "That's the kind of answer I would expect from a five-year-old."

"I'd be careful about insulting me if I were you. Let me remind you that I still have your phone held hostage. I won't be held liable for what might happen to it through the night."

I scooted a little closer and turned my head towards her so that my lips were just about grazing her ear lobe. Her scent, subtle and sweet, fueled the fantasies already running through my mind. "There's only one reason why I haven't taken my phone back from you."

"And why's that?" Without meaning to, I had come to rest my hand on her upper thigh. I was about to apologize and withdraw my hand when I felt her legs parting, if only slightly. Whether she was consciously doing so or whether it was an automatic response from her body, I did not know.

"Because there are too many people watching. But if we were alone..."

"Could you pass the dressing?" I didn't take my eyes off of her as I passed the cranberry vinaigrette.

"What do you mean?"

"Oh, you know exactly what I mean."

She kept a straight face as she wiped her mouth with a napkin, but I could see the redness peeking out from her cheeks and creeping as far as the tips of her ears. "Excuse me. I need to go to the bathroom," she said as she pushed back her seat and left.

As I picked at my salad, I scanned the crowd, awaiting her return. When she finally reappeared, her face was no longer a rosy shade of pink.

"The line in there was ridiculous," she said. "I couldn't wash my hands for the longest time because everyone was touching up their makeup."

"Isn't that always the case in a woman's restroom?"

"I just don't understand the obsession with caking your face with foundation. There isn't a single guy on the planet who is going to think a girl really looks that perfect. Makeup is supposed to highlight the beauty you already have, not give you a brand new face."

"I couldn't agree more," I said. "I think it says a lot about a woman's character when they choose to embrace their natural beauty."

"Fuck natural beauty. I want those extra minutes of sleep in the morning. I don't have the time to wake up early just to paint my face and hope to impress some guy."

I laughed. "That's one way of putting it, but I don't blame you. Those few minutes of snooze time are the best rest you can ever get."

"See? You get it." She refilled her glass with water. "When does our food get here? I'm tired of staring at this plate of salad."

"Soon. The waiters came around and asked what everyone ordered. I took the liberty of ordering you the steak. It's much better than the herb chicken."

"Thanks." She took up her utensils and began cutting up the steak into bite-sized pieces.

Soon came dessert. "You know, I don't understand why couples still bother with a traditional wedding cake. Everyone likes the ice cream better than the cake itself."

"Speak for yourself. This is real buttercream and it doesn't get any better than that." She brought a bite of cake to her lips. The way she wrapped her lips around that fork got my blood pumping. She did it again while looking right at me. Oh, she knew exactly what she was doing, and it was working.

I tucked myself further into the table to hide what was growing between my legs. My pants felt significantly tighter just as soon as she grabbed the cherry off her plate and popped it into her mouth.

"Just remember, teasing is a two-way street." She left me with those words as she got up and joined the growing crowd now on the dance floor. She disappeared between all the moving bodies. Occasionally, I'd get a glimpse of her fiery hair but never the rest of her. It was probably better that I didn't because I didn't want to see her grinding up on some other guy. I left the table and wandered toward an open door, hoping for some fresh air. To my pleasure, beyond the door was a balcony. It was empty.

I took a seat in a wicker chair, looking out at the impressively kept lawn. Without my phone, I didn't quite know what to do with my hands. Maybe Poppy was right. Maybe I had some sort of unhealthy obsession with my work, but it was that obsession that had made me so successful in life. I had sought to earn everything I had – never expecting anything to come my way for free.

At the edge of the property, a string of lights twinkled, hanging from a cluster of grapevines. Seeing the miniature vineyard made me think of my grandparents. They had a similar vineyard in their backyard and every year I'd help harvest the grapes and turn them into wine. Doing so was far from easy but it was rewarding work and I was always paid with a glass or two of unfermented grape juice.

Then at the end of the day, Grandpa would build a great big bonfire and tell us stories about his youth and how he had come to meet Grandma. As they told it, they weren't very fond of each other in the beginning. Grandpa would even go so far as to say that Henrietta was the "best pain in the ass a guy could ask for." Grandma would always answer him with a slap on the arm. Their relationship had always been something I had aspired to achieve for myself but so far, I'd had little luck in finding the woman of my dreams – the one I'd spend forever with.

As I leaned back in my chair and closed my eyes, Poppy sprang into my head. It was like she was right there in front of me. Behind her, a scene began to materialize. It was my grandparent's home and the place where I had grown up. She was standing by the fireplace, her features illuminated by the warm glow. I came up behind her and wrapped a blanket around her shoulders. The thought brought a smile to my face because while I had only known Poppy for a few short hours, the idea of spending an evening in my grandparent's lakeside cabin with her felt like a dream. Now, if there was only a way to make that dream a reality...

5
___

POPPY

S ometime during the night, I had lost my heels. I hadn't
the slightest idea of where they might be, but I guess it
didn't matter all that much because my feet hurt way too
much to try and put them back on.

Thinking another drink might ease the pain, I marched
over to the bar. It was crowded as everyone took advantage
of the never-ending supply of cocktails that constitutes an
open bar. The wedding was far from over and some people
were already trashed out of their minds. As for me, I was
enjoying the buzz. I was never a fan of getting full-on drunk
but getting tipsy, that was a whole other story. It helped
loosen me up and it made dull situations a lot more fun.

"What will it be?" asked the bartender.

I giggled even though there was nothing to laugh at. "A
White Russian," I answered once I had managed to
compose myself.

A minute later, he handed it over. I took it with another
giggle. "Ah!" I exclaimed after taking a sip. "Nice and
refreshing."

I walked past the dancefloor and thought about

rejoining the bump and grind, but my feet really needed a break. Spotting the sway of some curtains, I came to the conclusion that a bit of fresh air would do me some good. If nothing else, it would help cool me off. All that dancing had really worked up a sweat.

Outside, there was a light breeze. It played with my hair, throwing it behind my shoulders. Originally, I had half of my hair in an updo but that was no longer the case. Somehow, all the bobby pins stabbed into my head hadn't been enough to keep the bun in place. Oh well.

With my drink in hand, I leaned against the railing, admiring the view. The lawn had been decorated with twinkling lights. It honestly looked like something straight out of a fairytale. Maybe I didn't like how Connor had flaunted his money, but I had to admit that if he was the one behind the venue, he had exceptionally good taste.

Standing there, I thought about what he had said. Was his comment about fitting the bill for the wedding really just a demonstration of brotherly love? It was hard to think that he had spent thousands of dollars just to make Jenna smile. Of course, he wanted to the recognition. Very rarely does someone perform a good deed just for the hell of it. But, at the same time, Connor kept coming off as a good guy. Yeah, maybe he was a workaholic and maybe he had to work on his manners but he didn't seem like a typical douchebag. In fact, there was something different about him – I couldn't really decide what it was but whatever it was, I liked it. So, why had I ended up avoiding him for most of the night? Because the moment he placed his hand on my thigh, my whole body had gone up on flames and I've never felt that way before. I guess you could say that I was being cautious because with a smile like his and a personality to match, I was bound to get myself in too deep.

I finished off my drink and spotted a hammock. Ah, the perfect place to throw up my feet and relax. I threw myself into it and closed my eyes, swaying gently from side to side, letting myself forget about everything that was on my mind. During the course of the night, there had been one thought that had haunted me – Connor. There was something about Jenna's half-brother that had me all riled up inside. It was physical, sure, I couldn't deny that. He was handsome and incredibly charming but it was more than that; it was the way he listened to me – the way he was always trying to make me laugh – the teasing back and forth in all our conversations. To be honest, I think he was managing to make me...giddy.

"Nice of you to join me out here." The suddenness of Connor's voice had me up in a jolt. The hammock lurched dangerously to one side, nearly throwing me to the ground. I held on for dear life and remained statue-still in an attempt to steady myself and keep from falling.

"What are you doing here? Following me again?" I hiccupped and once again found myself hanging on for dear life. Maybe getting into the hammock hadn't been such a good idea after all but it was too late now. There was no way I'd be able to get out without making a total fool of myself.

"Actually, I was here first. I've been here for most of the night."

"Really?"

"Mhm." He held the hammock steady and joined me so that it became more of a swinging chair. With his feet still planted on the ground, he controlled our back and forth rocking. "Believe it or not, I'm really not a fan of parties."

"But I thought that's what rich guys do."

"Maybe some but not all of them. I prefer peace and

quiet. I'd rather spend my evening by a crackling fire than deafened by horrible pop music."

"What kind of fire are we talking about here?" I don't know whether it was the alcohol in my system or what, but I was actually moving closer. There was this sort of magnetism in the air that was pulling us together. Could he feel it too or was it all inside my head?

"Doesn't matter. A fireplace or a bonfire would both work just fine. If it were a fireplace, I'd sit by the hearth with a hot chocolate in hand, and should it be a bonfire, there'd be no way I'd forget the s'mores."

"Who would have thought that you were the sensitive type?"

He shrugged.

"And what if I were there? What would you do then? What would burn hotter, the fire, or us?" My lips met with the side of his neck. "Because, you know, I wouldn't mind if we ditched this place and had a bit of fun."

"How much have you had to drink?" he responded at once.

"Enough," I replied and giggled.

"Then you don't really mean what you say." His voice was different. There was a heaviness to it and his shoulders had dropped an inch or two. "I should get you a bottle of water." He was about to get up, but I grabbed him by the wrist and pulled him back down.

"Stay."

He did not argue with me.

The silence helped to clear the fog that had settled around my mind. "Do you think I could tell you something?"

"Sure, what is it?"

"When Jenna got engaged, I was happy for her. She had

finally found a man that truly made her happy but at the same time, the news felt like a slap to the face. When we were in high school, we had this grand idea in our heads that we'd get married by the time we were twenty-five, at the latest. Jenna was off by five years, but I have no idea when my day will come or if it will come at all. The fact that I'm turning *thirty* this year, I just can't believe it." I glanced through the open door where the party was still in full swing. "And here's the really pathetic thing. Jenna and I made a pact that if we were both still single by the time we turned thirty, we would marry each other. There goes that. I guess I'll just go on being forever alone while Jenna enjoys married life."

"I hear married life isn't all it's cracked up to be."

"That's what people say just to make you feel better about being single." I fell back into the hammock and looked up at the stars. They no longer seemed quite so bright.

Connor continued to rock the hammock back and forth. It was so consistent and smooth that I felt my eyelids become heavy. I was on the cusp of falling asleep when he said something. "Hmm?" I asked, not having heard him properly the first time.

"I was asking whether you swung that way."

"Hmm?" I asked again but this time on account of my confusion.

"You just said that you had a pact to marry Jenna if you were both still single at the age of thirty. So, I was wondering if you swung that way."

"Are you asking me if I'm lesbian?" I raised an eyebrow while trying my best to keep a straight face. His awkwardness was about the funniest thing on the planet.

"I guess I am."

"Why do you want to know?"

"Well, what would you say if I took Jenna's place in the pact? We'll get married just as soon as you turn thirty."

"If this is your attempt to get into bed with me, there are easier ways of doing it. For starters, you could just ask."

He got off the hammock and down on one knee. "What do you say?"

"That you have completely lost your mind." I tried to get off the hammock as well but it wasn't a very graceful transition onto the ground. Somehow, he caught me by the waist, arm wrapped naturally around my body like he had held me in the manner a million times before.

I hiccupped and fell into his chest.

He held me a little closer. "Have I?" He tilted his head towards mine. "Because if you ask me, it isn't so crazy as skydiving."

"When you skydive, you get a parachute. I barely know you. Until a couple of hours ago, I didn't even know you were my friend's half-brother. I still have no idea how that works."

"It's a long story," he said, swaying from side to side. There was a slow song playing. He seemed lost in his thoughts.

"Connor?"

"Hmm?"

"What happens if I say yes?"

"Then I make it worth your while." We continued to dance under the stars. I dared to rest my head on his chest and close my eyes. I could just barely hear the beating of his heart – slow and steady. In the quiet that followed his answer, I imagined what it would be like to marry this handsome stranger. Would I feel the jitters of a bride? Would I have that *glow* or was that only a perk of marrying someone you loved? And what would happen after the exchanging of vows? Would we get along or would we fight like every other married couple?

"Tell me something."

"Depends on what you want to know." Connor reached his fingers to my cheek. They tiptoed along my skin before pinning a strand of hair behind my ear. I felt a tingle run through my body like a current, electrifying my heart into overdrive. Looking into his eyes made me feel like I was looking at an old friend. It was like we had known each other all our lives and we were just now reconnecting.

"Why are you single?"

"I could ask the same of you," he said without sparing a moment to consider his answer. "You act like you'll never get married, but I've seen the looks you've been getting. I don't think you'd find it very difficult to find a boyfriend."

I pushed off his chest and leaned against the railing. "Finding a boyfriend and finding a future husband are two entirely different things."

He stood beside me. "Well, my offer still stands and as I promised, I would make it worth your while. As soon as my grandfather retires, I'm due to take over his share of the family business and become the majority shareholder-"

"Wait, slow down." I hesitated with the current line of thinking, trying to understand where he was going with his ramblings. "I fail to see how your grandfather's retirement has anything to do with our supposed marriage."

"Well, he won't retire until he feels comfortable passing off the business to someone else."

I wasn't sure whether I was being made stupid by the alcohol or whether he was just talking nonsense. "Come again?"

"He wants to pass off the business to a married man."

"So, let me get this straight. You want to take over your

grandfather's business and you can only do so if you're a married man? What difference does being married make when running a business?" I turned to face him, not yet addressing the fact that he was proposing that we get married just for financial gain. More than that, I wanted to know the reasoning behind his grandfather's marriage requirement.

"He thinks that being married makes you grounded. You're more likely to think rationally when you've got a wife and family to consider with every decision." Connor shrugged. "Honestly, I think I'm running my own business just fine as a bachelor, but I can't seem to change his mind on the marriage thing."

I crossed my arms over my chest. The whole thing was strange, to say the very least, but then again, family politics were never a simple thing to navigate. "Alright, assuming this is true, and your grandfather really wants you to get married, why wouldn't you get with a girl you actually like? I mean, I could turn out to be the biggest bitch in the world and I'm just playing nice because it's my friend's wedding. Do you really want to take a gamble that I'm wife material?"

In an instant, I was in his arms. His eyes burned with conviction. There wasn't an ounce of doubt in his body and trust me, I could feel every inch. "I am."

He did not let me go and frankly, I didn't want him to. My pulse was quickening, and I had this crazy urge to kiss him and just go along with it. I mean, it would make one hell of a story for future children. "What's in it for me?" I asked, my voice husky with desire. The alcohol in my system paired with the proximity of our bodies was burning me up from the inside. "Why should I say yes?"

"How does a mansion sound? Palo Alto. It's a really nice neighborhood. And of course, as my wife, you'd be living there rent-free." He grinned. "Not to mention a complete housing staff."

"Housing staff?" I asked, feeling myself becoming high with the idea of mansion living. "And does this mansion come with a pool?"

"It comes with both a pool and a pool boy," he said. "All you have to do is say yes."

It can't be this simple, I thought to myself. *Handsome men don't just propose to complete strangers like this. And they definitely don't give away their mansions in the mix. There had to be some sort of catch to this whole thing.*

"Poppy? Do I have an answer?"

"There's something you're not telling me."

"I thought I was making myself very clear. We have to convince my grandfather we're married so he hands over the majority share of his company and if we manage that, you get a mansion."

"And why do you want his company when you manage a company of your own?"

"Because I want to stop a certain someone from getting their hands on it. They're sure to make a mockery of it and I just can't let that happen."

"Oh?"

"Long story."

"If I'm going to marry you then I need all the answers."

He raised an eyebrow. "So, does that mean you're considering it?"

"Perhaps."

He turned slightly so he had me pressed against the railing. I felt the air rushing out of my lungs as his face came closer to mine. I closed my eyes and leaned forward.

Crack!

All of a sudden I felt weightless. The railing was no

longer pressed against my back. Without its support, I lost my balance. I screamed as I felt myself falling.

This is it. This is how I die.

But I never did crash into the hard earth because Connor had managed to catch me by the wrist. He pulled me into the safety of his arms and kissed me. And what a kiss it was. I didn't know if the adrenaline pumping through my veins was due to the near-death experience or the heart-pounding dance our lips were playing at. He grabbed at my hair and held me even closer like he feared I would fall once more.

Oh, I was falling alright.

6

CONNOR

There was a hunger inside of me. It growled and clawed at my chest, begging for more. I slipped my tongue into Poppy's mouth. She greeted me with an eagerness that only heightened my excitement. Her body had become an inferno, burning me to the core but still, I did not let her go. I would kiss her until my lungs gave out if I needed to. A girl this sweet isn't one you can just let go of.

We fell into the hammock and still, our lips remained locked. She had her hands on my cheeks. My hands fell to her backside, daring to give her a squeeze. Something like a moan escaped into the kiss. I could feel the blood rushing into certain places. Positioned as we were, I was sure she could feel it, too.

I pulled away, lightheaded from the lack of air.

She grinned. "Damn. You're one hell of a kisser. Why didn't you tell me when you were making your proposal? It would have sweetened the deal."

"I know something that can sweeten the deal even more." Without thinking, I took her into my arms, holding her in a bridal carry. In that moment, I was hit with the image of us as partners, laying underneath the nighttime sky, pointing out all the different constellations overhead. We'd laugh and hold hands, confident that there was a future for us full of endless conversation and unforgettable adventures. It was crazy to think this way when I had only known Poppy for a couple of hours, but it didn't take a rocket scientist to figure out that she was different from most girls.

She liked to eat. She liked to laugh. She didn't take life too seriously. She was a free spirit just looking for a good time. And I wanted to be a part of that – to let my rigidness loosen up – to find freedom in her laughter.

And maybe it was too big a leap to think this way. Maybe that was why I had brought my grandfather into the picture. It was a crazy notion but it seemed to make more sense than to admit that maybe I was falling for this girl because such emotions aren't supposed to develop so quickly. It just doesn't happen.

So, why did I feel this spark? This connection of our heartstrings every time she told me something about herself?

She giggled. "Where are you taking me?"

"Are you staying at the hotel?" I asked.

"I think so." She pressed a finger to her temple, trying to think. "But I can't remember what room number I'm in. Maybe you could let me stay in your room?" She tugged on my tie, loosening it. I looked down at her and saw a certain glossiness in her eyes. She was still tipsy. Kissing her was one thing, but I wasn't about to score a run at her expense. I'd wait until she was sober. Besides, sex is so much better when both parties are active participants and I had a feeling that Poppy was one hell of a firecracker in bed.

"Connor?"

It was Jenna. "Oh, hey, Jen." I tried to sound casual even though I held her friend in my arms.

"Jenna!" Poppy leaped forward and by some miracle, she managed to land on her feet. "One hell of a brother you've got here. He just saved my life."

"How much has she had to drink?" Jenna whispered in my direction.

"I'm not entirely sure, but I was planning on getting her back to the hotel room."

"Good idea. She's a liability whenever she's even a little bit tipsy. Honestly, I've never seen such a lightweight."

"Hey! Who are you calling a lightweight?" The pout on Poppy's face just made her look a thousand times cuter. "I'll have you know that I'm completely in charge of my faculties."

"Of course, you are," I whispered into her ear, lips grazing against her lobe. She became stiff. I heard the hitch of her breath against the back of her throat. The DJ had finally finished playing his infernal playlist and was packing up for the night. "Come on, the party is over."

Outside, we waited for the shuttle that would take us to the hotel. Poppy rubbed her arms. I took off my suit jacket and draped it over her.

"I really don't understand you," she said.

"Why's that?" I asked.

"You're this drop-dead gorgeous guy who owns a successful business, that's one thing. But then you come at me with a sense of humor. I'm not saying you're perfect, but you've proven you can be pretty damn sweet. I've smiled more today than I have in a long time. I can't let myself believe that you haven't made other girls feel this way. So, why the hell are you asking me to marry you?"

"That," I said. "That right there." I kissed the top of

her head and spoke the words that had been on my mind all day. "You're different. You'll actually say what's on your mind – maybe with a little coaxing, sure," I said, remembering the hiccup where she thought I was flaunting my money like some sleaze. "But I value honesty in a person and I can tell you're not the kind of girl to tell a lie."

"Oh, I know how to lie," I said. "Come Sunday, I can lay in bed all day!"

I chuckled. "That's a good one, but you might want to work on your execution. You messed up your tense there."

"Oops."

POPPY STOOD in the middle of my hotel room looking like she had been struck by a truck. Her jaw hung agape as she took in the sight of the crystal chandeliers and the 72-inch TV above the fireplace. "I don't even want to know how much you're paying for a room like this."

I shrugged. Poppy had made it clear that she didn't like it when I showed off my money and that was perfectly fine with me. "Can I make you some breakfast?"

"Breakfast?" she asked. "What time is it?"

"Quarter past three," I answered.

Her eyes widened. "Jeez. I had no idea it was so late. Usually, I'd be passed out in my bed at this hour, but I'm wide awake." She took a seat at the kitchen island while I turned on the coffee machine. I checked the mini-fridge and found some yogurt. On the counter sat a gift basket complete with biscuits and aged meats.

"Help yourself," I said.

"You sure? Hotels usually rip you off with this stuff."

I answered her by biting into a chocolate-filled croissant.

"Right." She grabbed a package of saltines. "Mind if I turn on the TV while the coffee brews?"

"Be my guest."

Her hips swayed from side to side as she made her way to the couch. Was she doing so on purpose? Was she trying to get me riled up? If it was intentional, it was working. I adjusted myself and tried to focus on working the coffee machine. It was one of those higher-end models capable of making espressos and cappuccinos. I looked around for a set of instructions but found nothing. I guess I was on my own.

Suffice to say, I wasn't used to making my own coffee. The first couple of attempts proved as much. The cappuccino came out pitch black despite the fact that I had opted for steamed milk. I tried again only to have the whole thing hiss like a feral cat. In the end, I managed to reset the setting to default and I settled for whatever the machine wanted to spit out at me. It certainly wasn't the best cup of coffee, but it was serviceable.

"Milk and sugar?" I asked but there was no answer. Glancing into the living room, I could no longer see Poppy. Perhaps she had gone into the bathroom.

I went to check but the door was open. I peeked into the bedroom next, but she wasn't there either.

Huh, I would have heard her leave, I thought. That's when I saw her passed out on the couch. She was holding one of the decorative pillows against her chest. I smiled at the innocence written on her face. Once again, I couldn't help but think that this girl was different. She didn't get on my nerves like most. I found myself wanting to be next to her just to share in her company. Why was I feeling this way? It was much too soon for these thoughts to be filtering through my head and yet, there they were because if being with her felt this good now, I could only imagine what the future would hold.

Gently, I slipped my arm underneath her and picked her up, careful not to wake her. She mumbled something before snuggling her head against my chest. For the second time that night, I kissed the top of her head. I don't know why but it felt like the right thing to do.

I laid her down in my bed and pulled the covers around her. I didn't think it would be very comfortable for her to sleep in her bridesmaid's dress, but I didn't want to put myself in a sticky situation by changing her out of it. I would have a lot of explaining to do in the morning.

Buzz!

At first, I didn't recognize the sound but then it dawned on me that my cell phone was still between her breasts. "Please, don't wake up," I whispered as I went for it. I held my breath, feeling like a jewel thief. At any moment I could touch one of those infrared tripwires and raise the alarms. I felt it between my fingers and grabbed hold, slowly wiggling it out of place.

Poppy went to turn over. Knowing I would get my hand trapped underneath her if she did, I pulled out as fast as I could. Thankfully, I was able to keep hold of my phone. I glanced at its screen. It was lined with notifications. I nearly checked them, my thumb hovering over the nearest one but then I thought against it. "Not tonight," I said as I threw it on the charger.

There was some moonlight coming through the blinds, illuminating Poppy's face. The sight of it took my breath away. To say she was gorgeous would be an understatement.

I thought about joining her, but I wanted to prove myself the gentleman. She was more likely to say yes to my proposal if she thought I was a good guy. So, I pulled up a chair and grabbed one of the books I had bought at the airport. I wasn't the least bit tired and it was difficult to think about sleeping when Poppy was the only thing on my mind.

You've lost your mind, came my voice of reason. *Proposing to a complete stranger. What are you, nuts?*

But I shoved aside these thoughts. I wasn't going to listen to them – not this time – because for once in my life, my heart spoke louder. I didn't quite know what it was saying but I knew well enough to listen.

Poppy snored lightly. It was a sweet sound. I chuckled. That was the thing about Poppy. She was *human – real*. She wasn't like all the other girls with their heaps of makeup and stiff curls. Poppy was authentic and unafraid to be herself. Even a single night with her had been enough to learn that. What I wanted, however, was to learn all the little details that made up her personality. What were her telltale quirks? Did she take her coffee black or was she a latte girl? Was she right-handed or left-handed? I wondered through the night, always looking up to make sure she was still real – that I wasn't caught up in some dream.

COME DAWN, I was drawn to the window. I hadn't slept a wink, but it didn't matter. Poppy was safe in my bed, sleeping the morning away. After hearing her cough a few times, I had been scared she would vomit in her sleep and choke on it, so I had moved her onto the side. I had even slipped the decorative pillow between her arms, so she had something to hold. The pillow seemed to do the trick because she didn't stir for the rest of the night. So, she liked to cuddle, then. Good to know.

I looked back but her face was buried. All I could see was the halo of her hair, messier than ever. I smiled, thinking of how I could make it look positively *wild*.

Outside, the sun was cresting over the horizon, painting the landscape with the same fiery red as Poppy's hair. I was usually so busy with work that I had never really stopped to admire a sunrise. I had thought it overrated and a waste of time, but now I saw how wrong I truly was. It was mesmerizing. In those moments, I forgot about everything else.

"Morning." Poppy was rubbing her eyes, blankets drawn up around her. "Have you been up long?" she asked.

"I never slept," I answered.

"Huh?" Poppy saw the light coming through the window. "But, it's morning, isn't it?"

"It is." I sat down on the edge of the bed. "I wasn't sure how much you had to drink, and I wanted to make sure you'd be okay."

"I just had a couple of cocktails," Poppy replied as she stretched out her arms. "You didn't have to worry."

"Better safe than sorry. I would really hate to lose the opportunity to slip a ring on your finger."

Her eyes widened. "So, that whole conversation actually happened? It wasn't a dream?"

"No, it wasn't a dream."

She pushed off the covers and looked down at her dress as if she were expecting something else. Her brow twitched slightly.

"Poppy?"

"You stayed up all night to make sure I was okay?"

"You sound like you're surprised."

"I kind of am," she said. "Most guys aren't so...considerate."

"I'm not most guys."

"I can see that." She flashed a smile. "You know, the idea of becoming your fiancée is getting rather tempting. But there is one thing I have to figure out first."

"And what might that be?"

In an instant, she was upon me, arms flung around my arms. She kissed me with a passion that was even hotter than the night before. It sent my blood racing through my veins, awakening the hunger I had felt on the balcony.

Her teeth nipped at my bottom lip, pulling gently while her eyes burned with her every intention. "Take a wild guess."

7

POPPY

I had promised myself some fun at Jenna's wedding. Maybe I was a day late, but I was still going to cash in on that promise. I owed it to myself. I hadn't felt the heat of someone's body against my own in much too long.

Connor threw me onto the bed. He pinned my arms above my head. "I've got a few ideas," he growled, going for the side of my neck.

I turned my head, exposing more of my skin. His lips traced out a path to my ear. He bit down on the lobe while his hand slipped under my dress.

My legs came apart, eager for his touch.

His fingers found my slit, not yet wet but quickly getting there. "Oh, and here I was thinking you wanted me..." He pinched my clit, rolling it back and forth. I pressed my hips into the air but for some reason, that made him stop. There was a devilish grin on his face. This guy was a teaser. Well, two could play at that game.

I pushed him off of me and straddled his hips like I was ready to ride him into next week. Matching his grin, I slowly unbuttoned his shirt. His chest was chiseled with muscle as hard as a rock. I traced his midsection. "Don't you know that good things come to those who wait?"

"I'm a very impatient man," he said, pulling down the zipper of my dress. "When I want something, there's nothing that can stop me from getting it."

"Then prove it."

And he did.

With my chest exposed, his mouth found my nipple. His tongue flicked back and forth, occasionally circling around it. I threw my head back, goosebumps covering most of my body for I had never felt anything like this before. His touch was divine. My thighs quivered and we were only at the start.

I had wanted to figure out whether we shared any chemistry. I think the answer was now obvious. At least as far as the bedroom is concerned, we were made for each other.

He took control, attacking my other breast with his teeth, marking his conquest.

I did the same, raking his back with my nails, leaving red lines that would tell the story of our lust. Somehow, we had gotten rid of our clothing, strewn all across the room. My panties had been ripped right off my body. Looks like I would be leaving the hotel room commando.

The morning sun lit up the room. I took in the sight of Connor's naked body. My body mounted. I had never scored this good before.

He paused, hand on my cheek. "You sure you're okay with this?" he asked. "All you have to do is tell me and I'll stop–"

I kissed him before he could say anything else. I could appreciate what he was doing, but the last thing I wanted was for him to stop. The sparks were flying, and I was ready for an all-out fire. I pulled him in with my legs, locking around the small of his back. There was no way I was letting him go. Our eyes connected in silent understanding.

He pressed himself against me. I felt him throbbing.

I reached down and wrapped my hand around his base. He was much thicker than I thought and as I slid my grasp along his length, I discovered he was much longer, too. "Someone's packing," I whispered, my voice raspy. "With a tool like that, what are you waiting for?"

Suddenly, there was something inside me but it wasn't his cock. Two of his fingers were pumping in and out. His thumb found my clit, rubbing it in circles. I cried out, shaking. Maybe I was out of practice, but I couldn't remember anything ever feeling this good and this was only the appetizer. I could only imagine what would happen during the main attraction.

"You're going to regret all this teasing." My legs tightened around his waist as I tried to grind into his length.

"Maybe that's what I'm hoping for." He added another finger, twisting them around, searching for my g-spot. This guy certainly knew what he was doing. "Maybe I'm just winding you up so you can do some bad, bad things to me."

"Careful what you wish for." Using my legs for leverage, I flipped us around. Once he was on his back, I got between his legs, crawling forward, back arched, ass swaying from side to side. I loved that he couldn't keep his eyes off of me. There was a hunger in his eyes, but he kept it in check, seemingly wanting to know what I would do.

Everything.

I wrapped my lips around him first. Then my tongue came into play, as I swirled it around the tip. He twitched inside my mouth just as soon as I squeezed his balls. I guess he wasn't expecting me to be quite so bold on our first night

– or rather, morning – together. But I wanted Connor to remember me. I wanted to go down as the girl who had blown his mind and left him a melted pile of putty.

Slowly, I eased down his length until he was pressed against the back of my throat. I paused and tossed him an innocent look like I didn't know what to do next.

His fingers found their way into my hair, encouraging me to keep going – to get right down to the base, but I wasn't going to give him that satisfaction just yet. I still had to pay him back for all the teasing. It was only fair.

I pulled back. He groaned and bit his bottom lip, clutching at the sheets. As soon as he pressed his hips into the air, I made my move, licking every inch until he was slick with my saliva. I took my time, tickling those most sensitive areas with the tip of my tongue. His eyes were starting to roll into the back of his head and his toes curled up. Nothing feels quite so good as knowing you have complete control over someone. I continued my dance, pushing him to his breaking point.

He shivered. That was my cue. I sat up and took him in both my hands, sliding them together, up and down, faster and faster.

"Fuck." He threw his head onto the pillows. He was pulsating in my hand, ready to blow.

"What's the matter?" I asked, my voice sweet, matching the innocence of my eyes. Not for a second did I stop pumping my hands. A drop of precum gathered at his tip.

Suddenly, he threw me off. I landed on the edge of the bed.

He was rummaging through the nightstand. I saw the silver-colored wrapper as he ripped it open. It fluttered to the ground as he rolled the condom onto his length. Then, his eyes met mine and I knew he was ready to play. He was on his feet, rounding the bed. With a tug on my ankles, he bent me over the mattress, my ass in the air. It was exactly what he wanted. Wasting no time, he took me from behind, pumping his hips hard and fast until I could hear the slapping of his balls against my skin.

"Fuck!" I cried out, for there was just something about the position that was a thousand times better than missionary.

"Do you like that?" he whispered against my ear, his voice like the growl of a wild animal.

Before I could answer, he pulled on my hair – hard. I arched my back and felt myself tighten around his girth, making it impossible for him to pull out. We both came, bodies shaking with pleasure.

Panting, we collapsed onto the bed, looking up at the ceiling.

"So," he began, looking my way. "Did you figure out what you wanted to know?"

"Definitely," I answered with a grin.

8

CONNOR

I don't know when she fell asleep exactly but when I looked over, she was curled against my chest. Underneath her, my heart had finally calmed down. During our throes of passion, it had been on the verge of exploding through my ribcage. Honesty, this girl had a fire in her the likes of which I have never experienced before. I wouldn't be exaggerating if I said she blew my mind.

Gently, I rolled her off my body. I pulled the covers around her and tucked a strand of hair behind her ear. I found the base of her neck, my fingers tracing her collarbone to her shoulder where I planted my kiss goodbye.

Since my clothes were scattered all over the room and I was pretty sure Poppy had popped a couple of buttons tearing off my shirt, I decided on wearing a whole new outfit.

Knowing I had errands to run, I opted for something a little more casual. I was still wearing a dress suit but today my sleeves were rolled back. Rumor has it that girls dig the look. I could only hope Poppy was one of them.

After adding some product to my hair, I left a note for Poppy, telling her to stay put until my return.

As I waited for the elevator, I began to whistle, and I never whistled. Poppy had definitely put a pep to my step. I felt like an entirely new person. Part of me considered turning around and starting up round two, but the thought of Poppy's sleeping face made me stop in my tracks. I wouldn't have the heart to wake her.

So, I took the elevator to the garage and jumped into my rental. I put the top down and enjoyed the seaside breeze as I drove into the city.

Halfway there, my phone started ringing. I expected a business call, but I was surprised to see Jenna's name pop up on the caller ID. "What's up?" I asked, answering through the car's Bluetooth. "I'm surprised you're up so early. Frankly, I think your husband may have missed the mark—"

"Don't," snapped Jenna. "I did not call you just so you could tease me about my wedding night."

"Then to what do I owe this pleasure?" I asked, trying to keep the amusement from my voice. The best thing about Jenna was that she was so easy to mess with.

"How's Poppy? I've been texting her all morning, but she won't answer."

"She's fine."

"So, you got her back to her hotel room last night? You made sure you got her into bed."

"You could say that." I checked the rearview mirror before changing lanes and stepping on the accelerator.

"What's all that wind? I can barely hear you!"

"I'll text you later." I clicked off the call and continued to cruise along the highway, using the time to think. There was no denying that Poppy was a hell of a time, both inside and outside the bedroom, but had I gone too far by proposing? And what did it say about me that I was willing to deceive my grandfather to get the family business under my thumb?

It's for the best, I told myself. If I wait to find my dream girl and marry in earnest, then it might be too late. If Neil beats me to it, he'll drive the Dresden name to ruin and I won't stand for it even if it means faking my own wedding.

With this thought in mind, I weaved through city traffic, following the GPS. There was something about islanders – none of them knew how to drive. Getting through a green light is like watching a snail crawl through molasses. Give me New York hustle and bustle any day.

I tried to make the light, but it turned yellow with a car still ahead of me. Since they weren't bold enough to go for it, I was made to wait another minute. Yes, I'll admit it, I'm not a very patient person.

Finally, I turned into the parking lot and took the spot right in front of the door. The security guard buzzed me in. I walked in, greeted by bright lights and a dazzling display of diamonds.

"How may we help you today?" The man behind the counter was a clean-cut gentleman with kind, grey-colored eyes.

"I'm looking for an engagement ring."

"Ah," he said with practiced interest. "Right this way. I think you'll find that our selection is next to none." He procured a set of keys and opened the case. He considered the rings for just a moment before pulling out one set with white gold and an almost obnoxious center diamond. "This style has been very popular as of late. The slight tinge of blue you see is a very rare quality."

I shook my head. "I would prefer something a bit more

classic in style – maybe even vintage. I'm thinking a 1950s vibe."

"Very good taste," said the jeweler. "We can certainly find you a piece and if there is nothing here to your liking, we can have something custom made."

"I'm afraid it is vital I leave here with a ring." I knew if I didn't, there was a chance I would back out of the engagement. For one thing, I didn't want Poppy slipping away, and for another, I prided myself on being a man of my word.

"Certainly." The jeweler led me to another part of the store. "How long have you two known each other?"

"A day," I answered.

His mouth hung open like a fish gasping for water. "A day?"

"Mhm. We met at my sister's wedding."

"And you've decided to get married yourself?"

I smiled at the jeweler. "I'll take this one."

He did not argue with me. He simply took my credit card and ran it through at the register. I didn't bother to look at the price tag. It really didn't matter whether the ring was $2,000 or $20,000. The whole arrangement was an investment and being a good businessman, I was sure to get a return on my money.

"Thank you." I tipped my head at the jeweler before taking my leave. Once in the car, I slipped the ring into my pocket. It felt strangely heavy. Was it the weight of what I was about to commit myself to? I pushed the thought aside and took towards my next stop.

It was a small boutique with raving reviews. Hopefully, their staff would help me pick out a replacement dress for Poppy because I didn't think she'd be wearing it again. Like her, I had been a little too eager.

"Hello, welcome to *Chrysanthemum!* Shopping for anyone in particular?"

"As a matter of fact, I'm looking for a dress my fiancée can wear to dinner tonight. Well, soon-to-be-fiancée." Her eyes widened just as soon as I showed her the ring. "I got my answer last night, but I'm an old-fashioned guy and I want to do it by the books and put an actual ring on her finger."

The girl clapped her hands together. "Oh, isn't that romantic! And the ring? It's gorgeous." She swooned, her eyes becoming dreamy. "I wish I could be so lucky." She batted her eyelashes as if that might make me change my mind, but she paled in comparison. Poppy was a flame like no other. "Anyway, let's get to that dress. Did you have something specific in mind?"

"Red. A-line. Maybe with a belt around the middle to accentuate her waist. Nothing too fancy as far as patterns go."

"You certainly know what you want."

"Always."

IT WAS STILL a little early for lunch but already I felt the tug of hunger. It was fed by the sight of the hotel staff rolling trays of food from the kitchen to the lunch buffet. It wouldn't open for another thirty minutes.

I rode the elevator up to the top floor, still thinking about food. I was in the process of looking up some good lunch spots when I walked into my room and saw Poppy on the couch. She was flicking through the channels wearing nothing but a bathrobe. But the robe wasn't even tied off in the middle.

"I tried finding one of your shirts, but it would seem you

didn't think to pack any of those oversized ones. I have to say, I'm a little disappointed. I was looking forward to playing the part of movie star." She stretched out and feigned a yawn.

Food was no longer on my mind.

I dropped everything by the door and dashed for the couch. She was quick, darting out of the room. I found her in the bathroom. "You can't hide from me in there," I said, closing in.

She shrugged off the robe and walked into the shower. "Who says I'm trying to hide?"

This girl was something else.

I struggled with my clothes as my mind struggled to function in the presence of such an attractive woman. She only made things worse by letting the water drip down her body, her hands following with a bar of soap.

Finally, I undid my belt and dropped my pants.

"I'm getting awfully bored in here, Connor. Weren't you taught that it's rude to keep a girl waiting like this?"

Her voice was like honey, echoing through the shower. I yanked open the door and quickly had her pushed against the wall, lips already on her neck as I hardened between her legs.

"Oh, how nice of you to join me," she purred, fingers running along the curve of my spine. "Where have you been all this time? You don't know how lonely I've been without you." Her pout was irresistible.

I kissed her. My tongue was quick to find the inside of her mouth – to explore more deeply what I had rushed through before.

She pulled at my hair and wrapped one leg around my waist. I took it as an invitation to lift her off the ground. I slammed her into the wall with another kiss for I could not get my fill of her. She was a sweetness that called for more – much more.

I broke off to catch my breath. "I'm here now," I said.

"Then let's make the most of it." Poppy took my hardening cock in her hand and gave it a few strokes before lining it up with herself. She dared me with a smirk, and I wasn't about to disappoint a look so demanding.

I pushed myself into her depths, struggling to get past her initial tightness.

The water suddenly felt hotter against my skin as her velvet insides quivered around me. Already, she was building me up. I wouldn't last long if I got down and dirty from the start. To keep this vixen as wet as possible, I needed to pace myself – to enjoy the scenery as it was laid out before me.

Her nipples were hard – maybe even harder than the diamond set within her engagement ring. I smirked at the thought and planted kissed all around her areola, teasing her a bit.

She tried to get some momentum going herself, but she couldn't move very much when I had her so firmly pressed against the wall. "You're mine," I growled right before biting down on her nipple. Her scream sent a jolt of excitement through my thighs. Unable to hold back any longer, I began to rock into her, taking it slow at first, letting the friction build alongside the lust we both felt.

Steam filled the bathroom. Our moans were muffled by the sauna-like atmosphere.

She steadied herself against my shoulders, shaking like a leaf. Knowing it would push her off the edge, I slipped my hand between her legs, finding her clit. I didn't bother easing her into it because I wanted to hear her scream and I wanted to hear it *now*. I rubbed her just as fast as I could.

Her nails dug into my skin, but I didn't feel the pain. I was too hopped up on the adrenaline – too focused on making her feel good.

"Connor!" It was what I had been waiting for. She threw her head back, eyes rolling. I held her by the ass, managing a few final thrusts before pulling out at the last second. It took everything I had just to keep standing.

She laughed. "You've made quite the mess."

"Good thing we're in the shower," I said with a wink.

Slowly, I set her down. The blood was slowly returning to other parts of my body but still, I felt lightheaded. Poppy was good – too good.

I took down the showerhead and adjusted the water temperature so it was perfect. Only then did I wash away my cum. With it gone, I took the liberty of washing the rest of her body, soaping up every inch of her gorgeous body. Just when I thought things couldn't get any better, she returned the favor.

9

POPPY

Sex with Connor was better than expected. There was an animalism about him that just got me going. He was irresistible in every way. Part of me still had a hard time believing we had done it *twice*, but there was no denying the wetness between my legs or the tingle in my thighs.

"That was amazing." Connor and I had migrated onto the couch. He had his arm around me while I cuddled against his chest.

"You're telling me," I said with a sigh. "Hey, do you think I could ask you something?"

"Sure, what's on your mind?"

"Well, from everything you've told me you don't get along very well with your brother, but I really don't understand that. I mean, I'm an only child. I wanted nothing more than to have a sibling when I was growing up and then my dad passed away and that was no longer a possibility."

"Your dad passed away when you were a kid?" he asked with a voice as gentle as the summer wind. "I had no idea."

"How would you? We only just met."

"And yet, I've asked you to be my wife."

I felt my breath catch at the back of my throat at his words. "You have, so I guess that means we will have plenty of time to get to know each other."

"We could start right now." He pulled me onto his lap and played with my fingers. "I'll tell you about my brother if you tell me something about your childhood."

"It doesn't have to be about my dad, right? His death isn't something I like to talk about."

"No, it doesn't have to be about your dad. I would never make you talk about something you weren't comfortable with. I just hope we can grow close enough to where you can tell me anything, even the things that bother you."

"I'd like that."

So, he told me all about growing up with Neil and how they were constantly butting heads and stealing toys from one another. Things only got worse when girls came into the picture. "You should have seen us in middle school. We were a couple of heart throbs."

"Did that last into high school?"

"Not in my case. Those were my nerdy years. I joined the robotics club and was pretty consumed with my studies."

"I wouldn't have pegged you as the nerdy type."

"Oh, definitely. I wore a pocket protector and everything."

"You did not."

"I did. I swear on the slamming sex we just had."

"Damn, so you're not lying then." We both laughed. "You know, this isn't what I think of when I think of post-sex conversation, but I kind of like it." I ran my fingertips along his arm. "And I guess it's only fair that I share an embarrassing detail from my adolescence."

"Indeed. I've been waiting. Don't hold out on me."

"Well, I can't give you the juiciest story just yet. How am I supposed to keep you interested?"

The rest of the night was spent sharing stories about our childhood. Some of them were embarrassing sure, but Connor made it easy to share things I would have otherwise kept to myself.

Hours later, I heard my stomach rumble. "Hey, are you hungry?"

"Famished." He picked up the hotel phone from the coffee table. "Fancy some room service?"

"Only if ordering room service means I can keep wearing this robe."

"Actually, I was hoping you could try something on for me."

"Oh?"

I watched as he grabbed the bag he had dropped by the door. "I got this for you since I sort of ruined the zipper to your dress."

"You did? I didn't even notice." I sat up a little straighter, trying to see what was in the bag. To be honest, I was curious. What kind of taste did this businessman have?

He pulled out a red dress, 50s in style, and conservative in cut. It wasn't something I would have picked out for myself had I seen it on the racks, but with Connor holding it, there was a sudden allure to its simplicity. I felt the fabric. It was silky soft but with a bit of stretch – the kind of material that's well-made and durable.

As I shrugged into it, Connor helped zip up the back. I shivered as his fingertip traveled along the length of my spine. He pulled away, waiting for the reveal.

I spun around, holding my arms out like I was ready to get my picture taken by a magazine photographer.

His face told me everything I needed to know. His eyes were fixed to me like glue.

Swinging my hips from side to side, I stepped into the bedroom. There was a full-length mirror behind the door.

"Damn." I couldn't believe what I was looking at. I barely recognized myself. With my hair wet and wild and the dress flattering every curve of my body, I'd never looked sexier. I turned, admiring my backside. "Damn," I said again.

"I'm going to take that as a sign that you like it." Somehow, Connor had slipped into the room and he placed his hands on my hips, curling around my waist. "I think this dress was made for you." He kissed the side of my neck and if he wasn't careful, he would push us into round three and I wasn't sure whether either one of us could handle it. "There's something else I want you to have." He held up a pair of panties. "As I remember it, I ripped off your other pair."

"You've thought of everything, haven't you?"

"I have." He stepped back and when I turned around, he was down on one knee, holding a ring box in his hand.

I blinked, not quite sure what I was looking at. "What are you doing?"

"Isn't it obvious? I'm making good on my promise from last night."

The sight of the diamond ring made me dizzy because I had a feeling it was real. Had he really dropped a few grand to propose to someone he had only just met? Okay, maybe I had considered the idea when I was tipsy, but I hadn't been in complete control of my senses. And this morning? Well, it was amazing to say the least, both under the covers and during those sweet moments where we held hands and talked the hours away. He had made a pretty good case for himself, but even so, I hadn't thought he was being serious.

"Connor, I don't know about this..."

He frowned. "What do you mean? I thought we were in agreement."

"Well, to be fair, you can't trust anything I say when there's alcohol in my system."

"What about this morning?" he pressed. "You weren't tipsy then."

"I was just joking around! You brought me back to your hotel room. I thought we both had the same intentions." I felt the door at my back. "I mean, think about it. Tell me you think it's just as crazy."

"I never said it wasn't." He stood up and pocketed the ring. "But I am being serious about my offer. If we get my grandparents to believe our story, that mansion is yours, no strings attached. And if you decide you want to keep things platonic from this moment forward, I'll agree to it, but I have to admit, I would be pretty disappointed. You sure know how to turn some gears."

"You aren't half bad yourself." I could feel him reeling me in. He was certainly a charmer. No wonder he had done so well for himself in the business world. How could anyone argue with a face so disarming?

"Or, we can have some benefits attached, whatever you'd like. I'm pretty flexible and as we've seen, so are you." He punctuated his offer with a smile that sent my heart thumping into the next room. "Hell, if you find me so atrocious and you just want to get the hell away from me, we can get a divorce."

"And you'll still get to keep your grandfather's business?" I asked, remembering bits and pieces of the conversation I had with him out on the balcony.

"Depends on the contract, but I would make sure to have my lawyers add a clause stating that my grandfather cannot retract his decision if something were to happen between us."

"That sounds deceitful."

He shrugged. "All is fair in love and contracts."

"I don't think that's how the saying goes."

He shrugged again.

"But even if we get a divorce, couldn't it be years before your grandfather decides to hand over the company? I mean, he wants to hand it over to either you or your brother, whichever one married first."

"That's the gist of it."

"Well, if marriage is so important to your grandfather, I really doubt he's going to hand over the company at the first sound of wedding bells. He's probably going to want to get to know me and frankly, I'm a very shitty liar. I've been flossing twice daily because I can't bring myself to tell the dentist that I don't, and do you know how much I hate to floss?"

He laughed. "I don't think anyone likes to floss, but you don't have to worry. I'm sure my grandfather will adore you. What's there not to like?" He took my hand and pulled me into his lap. "And if this takes a couple of years of us being together, I wouldn't mind it. But if you decide to have someone else on the side, I wouldn't object so long as we kept up appearances around my grandfather." It was like he was negotiating some business transaction. This was just another day at the office for him.

"Wouldn't you feel bad about tricking your grandfather with a fake marriage?" I asked, trying to implore to his sense of decency. Surely, he had to understand that his plan was fundamentally wrong. "Please tell me you have a reason for wanting the family business so desperately, and it'd better be more than money or else I'm walking out that door and never looking back."

Connor sat down. "I just don't want the business to fall into the wrong hands."

"Who else would it go to if not you?"

"I have a twin brother."

"A twin brother?" My expression became one of suspicion. "So, you're telling me that Jenna has yet another half-brother?"

"She does."

"Then, why wasn't he at the wedding?"

"He's not the most...reliable person." I could tell Connor was holding his tongue. "We don't always see eye to eye. When our mother died, our grandparents took us in. They're hardworking people and tried to teach us the same values. Back then, I used to work my ass off for chore money. Neil, on the other hand, did everything he could to get out of it. He hates lifting a finger to do anything, but he loves spending money, only it's never his money. As soon as he turned eighteen, he spent all of the inheritance our mother had left behind. Meanwhile, I invested it in my company, growing what I have now. I thought that alone would prove to my grandparents that I was the right choice when handing off the family business, but they are adamant about this whole marriage thing. And I really don't think Neil is beyond getting married just to sell the whole operation and make a quick buck."

I listened to Connor's story, trying to spot a lie. He sounded convincing and honestly, I was starting to dislike this Neil character, too. "Tell me more about this family business."

"My grandfather owns a lumber company in Maine. He

started off as a lumberjack right after serving in the army. Eventually, he became friendly with my grandmother who worked as a receptionist. Together, they rose through the ranks until they had finally saved enough money to buy the whole company outright from the owner. The owner was delighted since he and his wife did not have children." Connor paused. He got up and took both my hands. "Their story has always inspired me and if nothing else, I want to keep their legacy alive because if Neil manages to get his hands on that company, it'll be gone."

"How do I know you're not lying?" I asked.

"That's for you to decide."

"Mind if I think it over?"

"Of course." Connor patted his pocket where the outline of the jewelry box could be seen. "I have a thirty-day return on this thing, although I'd really prefer an answer sooner rather than later." He brought my hand to his lips and smiled that irresistible smile of his. "In the meantime, let's grab some lunch."

AFTER ORDERING LUNCH, we ventured out of the hotel room for some ice cream. I felt overdressed but honestly, I didn't mind it. My confidence was through the roof.

"What are you getting?" I asked as we got in line.

"I'm a man of classic taste," he answered. "So, it'll be one hot fudge sundae for me."

"Make that two," I said.

He slung his arm around my waist like we were a real couple just going on a typical date. "You know, if this works out between us, I don't think we'd make such a bad match."

"Speaking of which, I've been thinking, and I've come to a decision." We stepped forward, getting closer to the window. In front of us, a little kid was on tippy-toes, trying to see all the different flavors he had to choose from. All he had to do was pick whether he wanted rocky road or cookies and cream and if he didn't like his choice, he could always get something different the next time his parents brought him to the ice cream parlor. As for me, my decision to marry or not marry Connor was much more impactful. On one hand, I'd be helping to keep a family business alive but on the other, I had no idea whether I would be happy as Connor's wife or whether I'd be able to live with myself knowing I had bamboozled a couple of grandparents, never mind keeping up that facade.

What it really came down to was a gut feeling and my gut was telling me 'go, go, go.' Why? I have no idea. Marrying a stranger was completely outside my comfort zone, but I think that was the whole thrill of it. I wanted to unravel this mystery – to be a part of it. Besides, I was single and had been so for a long time now. I was due for a change.

"How long are you going to keep me in suspense, or have you changed your mind about the hot fudge sundae?" He snapped his fingers in front of my face. Apparently, I had zoned out looking at the menu board.

"Sorry." I was about to answer him, but it was our turn at the counter.

"We'll have two hot fudge sundaes."

I nodded in agreement.

With sundaes in hand, we made our way to the shade of a nearby palm tree. I leaned against it, taking my first bite. "Mmm, this is really good."

"I think it just tastes better because it's so hot."

"You might have a point." I took another bite, savoring

the thick layer of fudge. It was good fudge, too. I could tell it was made with real chocolate. "So, anyway, about the proposal."

The intensity of Connor's gaze made me a little nervous, but I wasn't going to put off my decision any longer. I wanted to stick to my guns before I could change my mind. "I'm headed back to Silicon Valley for a job interview. I'm hoping this becomes a career job for me, so it comes before anything else."

"I can understand that," he said.

"So, if I get the job, I'll take the deal. If nothing else, it'll save me a shit ton of money on rent."

Connor chuckled. "Not what I was expecting to hear, but I like the way you think. You'd make a good businesswoman."

"I considered it but too many sharks in the tank."

"That's the truth." He scraped at the bottom of his container, trying to get every last bit of fudge off the sides. "Well, if you getting the job is the determining factor, I'll have to put in a good word for you since I know everyone in the industry."

"No," I said at once. "Don't. If I get this job I want to get it on my own merit. I don't want handouts."

Connor smiled knowingly. "A woman true to my own heart." He pulled out the ring box. "In the meantime, would you consider wearing the ring?" Before I could even think of responding, he had the ring on my finger. Like the dress, it was the perfect fit – like it was made for me no one else. I turned my hand. The center diamond glittered in the sunlight.

"You make it really hard to say no."

"That's the name of the game," he said with a wink.

10

CONNOR

I dropped by Poppy's hotel room the following afternoon, but it was being cleaned. It appeared Poppy had already checked herself out. I felt slightly disappointed that she hadn't called, but she had the right to travel on her own if that's what she wanted.

So, I got in my car and drove to the airport. While everyone was waiting in lines, I zipped right through with my TSA pre-check. Honestly, I did not pity anyone going through security. That is until I saw Poppy holding her sneakers in her hands and shuffling towards the metal detectors, a defeated, almost dead look in her eyes.

I stepped out of line, letting other well-to-do people cut in front of me, and dialed Poppy's number. The result was comical. Poppy had no idea where her phone was. First, she checked her purse and then her backpack. She dropped her sneakers and nearly knocked over a small child with her luggage bag. The parents of said child had some choice words to share. Clearly, they did not care about setting an example for their son.

Poppy apologized profusely as her phone continued to blast its ringtone.

Having laughed at her expense long enough, I decided to whistle. That got her attention. "Connor?"

"Need a hand?" I picked up her sneakers and grabbed her luggage.

"Excuse me, what is going on here?" A stern-looking TSA officer approached us. With a motion of her finger, she had us step out of line. Poppy looked dismayed, fearing she would get sent to the back of the line.

I held up my pre-check card as if that were answer enough. "I want to take her along as my guest."

The TSA officer crossed her arms. "Only passengers under the age of thirteen can accompany a pre-check member. Unless she has a pre-check card of her own, I cannot let her through."

I furrowed my brows together. "Even if she's my fiancée?" I held up her hand to show off the ring on her finger.

"She could be the Queen of England for all I care," said the officer. "No card, no go."

I was stumped. Given, I had never tried to bring a guest through the express land. I rarely traveled with a companion and when I did, it was usually another businessman with a pre-check card of his own. More than that, I was amazed there was actually an airport employee trying to do her job.

"Back of the line, you two."

I was about to argue with her, but Poppy took me by the crook of the arm and towed me away. "I'm going to miss my flight because of you. I'm late enough as it is," she hissed just as soon as we were back in line. "Why the hell did you have to make a scene? I was almost at the metal detectors; now I have to wait all over again."

"I honestly thought I could bring a guest through the express lane."

Poppy pinched the bridge of her nose. "Don't you think that would open up the door for a whole bunch of security breaches? I mean, they pre-approved you, but what's stopping you from bringing a criminal on the plane?"

She had a point.

"Well, don't just stand there."

"Hmm?"

"You have to take off your belt and shoes."

"Right." It had been so long since I had been forced to go through the motions that I was a little out of practice. "This is a pain in the ass, isn't it?"

"Why do you think everyone complains about going through airport security? It isn't a walk in the park." She handed me a plastic container. "Put everything in there and slide it down the belt.

"Sir, is there anything in your pockets?"

"My keys," I answered the officer, who was wielding a scanner.

"Those go in a container," he said, his tone clipped with impatience. The people behind me groaned as I struggled to comply with the rules. It seemed ridiculous that I needed empty my pockets of *lint*. Whoever heard of explosive lint anyway?

Finally, I made it through, feeling like some sort of circus monkey who had just been put on display for the last hour. "That was ridiculous," I said, joining Poppy on a nearby bench. She was struggling with untying her shoelaces. Without thinking, I took the sneaker from her and worked on the knot.

"Last call for Flight 72B for San Jose International Airport."

"Shit! That's me!" Poppy grabbed all of her belongings and started sprinting. I still had her sneaker in my hand, but she didn't seem to have any intent on coming back to get it.

Shaking my head, I followed her. Flight 72B was leaving out of Gate A18 which was in the west wing of the airport. Poppy had gone running in the opposite direction. I thought about calling her and letting her know, but given the fact that she had yet to locate her phone within the mess of her pocketbook, it was probably best to just let her figure it out on her own.

Eventually, I found her slumped in a chair looking like she wanted to scream. "Missed your flight?" I guessed.

"I couldn't find the gate and by the time I did, I was too late." She hung her head, rummaging through her things until she found a tattered paperback book. "Now I'll have to book something with the next available flight and hope they have something available. Either way, I'll probably be here a while." She shot me a pointed look. "This wouldn't have happened if you had just let me go through security. Why did you have to show off your pre-check or whatever? I was perfectly fine on my own." With a huff, she started to march toward the nearest counter. I stopped her before she could get very far.

"Look, I was only trying to help you out back there. I had no idea we would get sent to the back of the line. In any case, don't bother buying a ticket for another flight."

"So, what, you want me to stay in this airport indefinitely?"

"We're both going to the same place. Why don't you hitch a ride with me? I won't even charge you."

Confusion swept across her face. "What are you talking about?"

"I'm talking about my private jet. There is more than enough room for two," I said with a sly grin."

"Fuck." She grabbed the bottle of water from my hand and took a drink to steady herself. "Alright, well, if it'll save me buying another ticket, I accept."

"I was hoping you would say that."

"Mind if we stop at the duty-free shop?" she asked.

I laughed. "You know the whole duty-free thing is a scam, don't you?"

"Yeah, but do you see the size of those chocolate bars?"

"THIS IS AMAZING. I still can't believe I'm on a private jet. This sure beats flying economy." She reclined her seat so that it was pretty much a bed and opened her paperback. The bookmark smacked her in the face.

I couldn't help but laugh. She scowled but it disappeared just as soon as I handed over a glass of champagne.

"How much did it cost you to buy this thing?"

"A good businessman never discloses his numbers."

"You aren't a magician."

"Give me a sum of money and I can make magic happen," I said.

"Care to take over my portfolio?" I knew she meant it as a joke but there was a hint of hopefulness in her voice. "Because right now it's dead in the water. I tried to tackle all the buying and selling myself, but the market is hard to predict."

"There's a reason why people hire investors." One of

the flight attendants came over with a platter of assorted cheese and crackers. "If you want something else, let me know."

She held up her oversized chocolate bar. "I think I'll be good for a while. Do you want a piece?"

I took the square from her palm and popped it into my mouth. It was sweet but not quite so sweet as the woman sitting across from me. I yearned to have her again, but the ball was in her court. If she wanted to take the proposal beyond just a matter of pretend, then that was her decision to make.

"The seat has a massage feature," I said as I turned on the flat-screen TV and searched for a movie I thought she might like.

"You're kidding me!"

"I'm not. There's a button on the remote."

She grabbed the remote, an excited smile spreading across her face. "Ahh," she moaned. "This flight just keeps getting better and better."

IF SHE HAD BEEN IMPRESSED by the private jet, she was blown away by the mansion. She stood in the driveway, mouth agape, and eyes wide. "So, if I marry you and you get majority share of your grandfather's company, I get to keep this place?"

"Free of charge."

"Pool boy included?"

"Pool boy included," I confirmed.

"Wow..." She stepped forward. Her face was clouded over in amazement. "I just can't believe it..." She reached out and touched the gold knocker. It was a piece imported from France. The lion's head was intricately carved with minute details only seen under a magnifying glass. She tried out the knocker. "It actually works."

"Of course. If you bang metal on metal, it usually makes a sound."

A member of the house staff answered the door, ushering us inside.

Poppy floated from room to room. Occasionally, she would touch something or ask me a question, but for the most part, she was silently taking in all the sights of her new home.

"Shall I show you to your room?" I asked as we approached the door.

She nodded.

"I hope you don't mind staying in the guest room," I said as she stepped inside.

"Mind?" She shook her head. "This room alone is almost as big as my place back in Atlanta." She draped herself in the curtains, dawning them like a cape. "And you're sure that you want to just *give* me this place if you get your grandfather's company?"

"I won't need it. I intend to move back to Maine. It's quieter there and I think I'm ready to settle down."

Poppy nodded. "Yeah, I can imagine how hectic it must be to deal with San Francisco living all year long. Although, I have to imagine it's better than New York."

"They both have their flaws, but I'd take San Francisco over New York, you're right."

She allowed herself to fall into the bed and become buried in the mountain of pillows. "I think it's time for a nap."

"I'll leave you to it then." I had the urge to kiss her

before leaving the room, but I decided it was still too soon for such gestures. Maybe, if I was lucky, the relationship would grow, but until then, I was okay with taking things one step at a time. I had gotten her to agree to the proposal, that was the first and most critical step. Everything else would follow.

11

POPPY

My nap turned into a full night's sleep. Despite the luxurious ride in Connor's private jet, I was still exhausted. I could feel it in my bones as I stretched.

Mmm, maybe a few more hours of sleep, then, I thought as I reached for my phone. *But what time is it?*

The brightness in the room was enough to tell me that at the very least, it was morning. Outside the window, I heard the twittering of birds and a faraway bark of a neighboring dog.

11:38 A.M.

"Damn, good thing my interview isn't until two," I mumbled to myself, trying to rub the sleep from my eyes. It was incredibly difficult to roll out of bed when the mattress felt like a cloud. I had half a mind to remain curled under the silk sheets for the rest of my days.

Still in the process of waking up, I checked my social media and saw that Jenna was having fun on her honeymoon. I was happy for her even though I was still a little upset that she had failed to tell me she had a pair of twin brothers. Then again, she hadn't been the type of girl to share much about her past and I wasn't the one to ask.

I caught sight of the ring on my finger. It felt strange to see it there. I slipped it off and studied it more closely. It was truly a beautiful piece and like everything else, it had probably cost Connor a fortune. At the wedding, I had thought him smug for showing off his money, but now I understood that he worked hard for every cent he made, and he was reaping the benefits of his labor. Could I really fault him for that?

Growing bored of my feed, I threw aside my phone and headed for the shower. It was even bigger than the one in Connor's hotel room and it had a built-in bench. I grinned, thinking of everything that could be done on that bench. Maybe there'd be time to test it out in the future because this proposal with benefits idea was starting to sound pretty grand. I didn't know whether Connor was the guy I wanted to spend the rest of my life with, but why should that stop me from having some fun along the way?

I turned the knob expecting water, but instead, I was met with steam. It filled the entire shower stall, thick enough to leave droplets of moisture on my skin. "Oh, this is nice," I moaned. "Really nice."

The shampoo was salon quality and the bar of soap was handmade from some goat farm. Connor really spared no expense when it came to quality of life items. I was starting to like his style.

Stepping out of the shower, I felt like I had dawned a new skin. I was glowing and my hair, even as wet as it was, looked healthier than ever. There was a robe hanging on the back of the door; I grabbed it and melted against its fluffiness. The steam from the shower had left the fabric warm.

I padded across the plush carpet and found the red

dress Connor had given me. I couldn't resist wearing it. Besides, the key to every interview is dressing your best and I definitely looked my best dressed in red.

Taming my hair was a different matter. Drying it makes it frizzy and trying to get it sleek and shiny took a whole lot of elbow grease. In the end, I gave up and decided to contain it within a bun. Thankfully, I had brought along plenty of bobby pins for the wedding. Satisfied that I looked like a professional, I finally ventured out of the bedroom.

In the hall, I noticed Connor's door had been left ajar. Curious to see his room, I peeked my head through the crack. It was even bigger than the guest room. A four-poster bed made of solid wood dominated the space. The carvings made the whole thing look regal in nature like it had been crafted for a king.

"Ahem."

I nearly jumped right out of my skin. Turning around, I saw a member of the house staff standing in the hall, hands clasped behind his back. "Uh, sorry. I was just wondering whether Connor was still in his room. I wanted to have a word with him..." It wasn't really a lie. After my time in the shower, I was eager to see him. Although, talking wasn't exactly what I'd had in mind.

"Connor has left to tend to his affairs. He will not return until later this evening."

"Right."

"There is breakfast in the kitchen." He consulted his watch. "If you'd rather have lunch, that can be arranged."

"Brunch?"

"Brunch can also be arranged," he answered with a nod. "Please, follow me."

The kitchen was massive. A middle-aged man wearing a chef's hat was handling a flaming frying pan. He left it on the stove and proceeded to chop something with a knife about the size of my head.

"Wait, is all this food meant for me?" I asked seeing the buffet-like set up on the island. "This is enough food to feed a small nation."

"Mr. Dresden was not aware of what you preferred, so he told our chef to make a variety of dishes for you to choose from."

"I would have been perfectly content with a bowl of cereal..." I answered while rubbing the back of my neck. I felt awkward knowing the chef had gone through so much work just for my sake. It would be rude of me not to try a little bit of everything.

By the time I was done, I was stuffed. From the three-cheese quiche to the crème brûlée French toast, I would need to run a marathon to burn off all the calories. Even so, I was pleased. The food was exquisite, and far better than a plain ol' bowl of cereal. "Thank you."

The chef bowed and took his leave. Someone else materialized and cleaned up.

"Do you want some help?" I asked.

The girl shook her head. "No, please, don't worry yourself. It is my job." She smiled politely before loading up the dishwasher.

I sought the member of staff I had met in the hallway outside my bedroom. "I'm sorry," I said, "but I never got your name."

"Vernon," he answered.

"Vernon. I'll remember that." I nodded my head as if that might help me commit his name to memory. "Well, I was wondering if you know a good taxi company to call. I have a job interview in an hour, and I wanted to get there a little early so I could get a feel for the campus."

"There will be no need for a taxi," said Vernon.

I thought about the high heels I was wearing. There was no way I would be walking there.

"The chauffeur will take you wherever you need to go."

"The chauffeur?"

"Indeed." Vernon turned on his heel and proceeded to the front door. Dumbfounded, I followed. Even after spending a few days with Connor and riding in his private jet, it was still difficult to believe that I was being given access to something like a chauffeur. I mean, I was just a regular girl and regular girls do not get the luxury of being driven around by a man in uniform.

And yet, there he was, standing in front of a six-figure vehicle. Its white coat was inlaid with pearl, causing it to sparkle in the sunlight. Honestly, I didn't know what was brighter, the car, or the summer sun.

"Where to?" he asked, opening the back door with his white-gloved hand. This was the kind of treatment given to movie stars. Subtly, I pinched myself just to make sure it was real. The sharp pain told me I was awake. "*D & D Aeronautics*," I said. "Do you know it?"

The chauffeur chuckled. "Of course."

"Oh?" I was hoping he would let me in on the joke, but he did not say another word as he settled behind the steering wheel and took to the road.

I looked over my resume and prepared for the interview, but I only succeeded in getting inside my own head. Doubt crept to the surface and took hold of my nerves. *D & D* would never hire me. I had no experience in Aeronautics other than an avid interest in space documentaries. As for being a website manager, I had good references, but would they really make me stand out from the crowd? My stomach twisted into a knot as I considered the possibility of rejecting – of packing up my things and going back home to Atlanta – of leaving Connor and his mansion behind.

"If you want some water, help yourself." The driver broke through my thoughts.

"Oh, yes, thank you."

Thinking small talk might help get my mind off the interview, I leaned toward the partition that separated us. "Have you worked for Connor for long?"

"A few years now," he answered.

"And how is he? As an employer, I mean?"

He caught my eye in the rearview mirror. There was a look of amusement on his face. "He's mighty generous, especially during the holiday season. And when my wife had a baby he gave me three months of paid leave. Oh, yes, he's mighty fine. I'm sure you'll figure that out for yourself soon enough."

I didn't have the time to figure out what he meant by his final comment for we had arrived at our destination. My nervousness returned in full force. I swallowed back the rock in my throat.

You can do this. Just show them that you're the woman for the job, I told myself as I stepped out of the car.

"Best of luck," said the chauffeur as he handed me a card. "Just give me a call if you need a ride anywhere else."

"Thank you." I slipped the card into my purse and watched as he drove away. For a few minutes, I remained fixed on the sidewalk. It was like my legs had stopped working.

Finally, I took the first step and allowed myself to relax. What was the point in worrying? I was only making myself sick. Whatever happened, happened. I would just have to live with it and move on. Still, I kept my fingers crossed that all would go well.

The campus was bigger than I'd expected. There were multiple buildings and I wasn't quite sure which one I was supposed to go into for my interview and for the life of me, I could not find the email they had sent me with the instructions. Thanks, junk mail.

Taking a chance, I entered the building closest to me and was lucky enough to be met with a friendly receptionist. "Hello, I'm here for an interview with Ryan Baker. I know I'm a little early, but I'm not familiar with the area and I wanted to make sure I arrived on time."

"Not a problem," said the receptionist. Mr. Baker likes an early bird. You'll find him in his office. Let me give me him a quick buzz and see if he's ready for you now."

"Thank you."

I busied myself by looking around. The lobby of the building was of modern style. Glass displays showcased what the company was working on. Center stage was a model replica of a jet that looked a lot like the one I had ridden on. Had Connor bought his jet from *D & D*? Now wouldn't that be a coincidence?

"Miss?"

I turned around and saw that the receptionist had gotten to her feet.

"If you'll follow me, I'll show you to the elevator. You'll want to take it to the seventh floor. Mr. Baker's secretary will give you further instruction."

"Thank you."

"My pleasure." The elevator matched the modern style with its simple stainless steel doors. After a short wait, I stepped inside the cabin and rode to the top floor.

Breathe, Poppy, breathe, I recited in my head over and over again. It was all I could do to keep myself from getting off on an earlier floor and abandoning the interview altogether. I couldn't understand why I was so nervous. Usually, I was confident and surefooted, but there was just so much riding on this particular interview. Getting the job would mean a major overhaul in my life. I would be leaving my shitty Atlantic life for something better. My path to success started here and that's what made it so nerve-wracking.

Don't mess up, came that little voice at the back of my head. Yeah, well, easier said than done.

The seventh floor was clean and polished. A young woman sat behind a desk watering a succulent. She smiled at me. If nothing else, at least everyone at *D & D* seemed super friendly.

"Hello." I returned her smile and held out my hand. "My name is Pomona Merritt. I'm here for an interview with Mr. Baker. I believe the receptionist downstairs gave him a buzz to say I was here since I'm a bit early."

"Yes, of course. Right this way."

It was a short walk to his office. Unlike the rest of the building, it was cozy with an almost hippie vibe to it. There was some sort of rug hanging from the ceiling. It was odd but I sort of liked it.

"He will be with you in just a moment."

And just so. A well-dressed man with a head of cherubic curls walked into the room. He wasn't wearing any shoes. "It's a pleasure to finally meet you in person," he said. "I must say that you impressed me during our phone interview. This is really only a formality. I really have no doubt that you'll be hired today."

I felt a weight being lifted from my shoulders.

"Mr. Dresden will, of course, make the final decision, but we tend to be in agreement, and I cannot see how he should find fault with such an impressive resume." He had a copy of it on his desk. He glanced over it for only a moment. "You graduated with high honors, did you not?"

"I did."

"Well, I think you will find plenty of opportunity to grow here at *D & D*. It's a newer company but it's already making leaps and bounds in the industry. Some of the other tech giants are quaking, as they should." He came around his desk and sat down on the edge of it, looking me up and down with an expression that spoke of hunger. "Honestly, I think you'd be an excellent addition to the team."

"I hope so."

"So, have you been in the city very long?"

"Flew in yesterday after attending my friend's wedding in Hawaii."

"No kidding? Mr. Dresden just attended a wedding in Hawaii as well."

Strange, I thought.

"Maybe I could show you around the town sometime. There's a lot to see that won't ever get mentioned in those tourist handbooks."

Was this guy asking me out on a date?

"Uh..."

"There's this nice little Italian restaurant not far from here. Or, if you like Korean food–" He stopped in the middle of his sentence.

I looked up, wondering why, and saw that he was looking right at the ring on my finger.

"My apologies, I did not know you were with someone." His flirtatious tone had evaporated.

"It's sort of a long story..." I said, hoping that would be enough to get him off the topic. The office fell into an awkward silence. I fidgeted in my seat, growing uncomfortably hot in the thick material of my dress. "I don't believe you've given me a reason as to why I'm having my interview with someone else. Has there been a change of plans?"

"Actually, there has," he said, returning to his desk. "Mr. Dresden no longer wants a website manager."

"What?" I sputtered. This was a total screwball. After working my ass off to get a degree, I thought becoming the website manager would be my golden ticket – the entry point into a realm of possibilities. "What do you mean he no longer wants a website manager? Then why am I here?"

"Because a new position has opened up and Mr. Dresden believes you're just the person to the job."

My mouth went incredibly dry. I glanced around the office hoping to find a water cooler. "And what might this new position be?" I asked, trying to keep my voice as level as possible even though I was on the verge of a major freak out.

"Mr. Dresden would like a personal assistant."

"Personal assistant?" I asked, dumbfounded. "And what makes him think I would make a good personal assistant? I have absolutely no experience with any secretarial work and my degree is totally irrelevant to such a position." I got up, on the verge of pacing but I managed to keep still for the moment.

"The pay will be exactly the same and Mr. Dresden is even adding a few extra benefits, although he hasn't told me what these benefits are."

"When was this decision made?" I demanded. "Why wasn't I notified?"

"Yesterday." Baker sat up a little straighter. "Trust me, I found it just as surprising, but Mr. Dresden is the boss. I don't make the rules – I just follow them."

I was just about to decline the interview altogether when there was a knock on the door.

"Mr. Dresden is ready to see you now." It was the young woman from before.

I followed her in a trance-like state because my brain had stopped working. As we approached the end of the hall, I felt a seedling of curiosity start to grow in the pit of my stomach. There was definitely something odd about the whole situation and was part of the reason why I kept walking. I wanted to meet this Mr. Dresden and figure out why he had suddenly thrown a monkey wrench in my career plans.

So, once again I told myself to breathe and just roll with the punches.

But I wasn't expecting *this*.

12

CONNOR

"Connor?" Poppy stood at the door to my office looking like she had just been hit by a truck.

I kept the amusement from my face as I continued to pour myself a cup of coffee. "Would you like some?" I asked. "It'll only take a minute to brew."

"What are you doing here?"

"That's a funny question to ask of a CEO." Seeing as Stephanie was still lingering by the door, I dismissed her. "Please, take a seat."

"Is this some kind of joke?"

I returned to my desk and pitched my fingers together. Poppy was wearing the red dress I had gotten her, and it looked better than ever. "It would seem to me like someone failed to do their research when applying for the job. Usually, I wouldn't consider taking on someone who hasn't been thorough, but I think for you I can make an exception."

Poppy took a few unsteady steps toward my desk. A deep redness was climbing to the tips of her ears. The blush made her that look much cuter. Had the door to my office been locked, I would have tried something, but I knew the limits of my professional setting. Even so, there was nothing stopping me from *thinking* about Poppy bent over my desk, dress skirt hiked up and out of the way.

"I don't understand," she said, helping herself to a cup of water.

"Isn't it obvious?" I mused, revealing the grin I had been trying so hard to conceal. "I'm Mr. Dresden."

Her eyes widened with realization. "Wait... so you knew..."

"Of course. There aren't many people named Pomona." My grin deepened. "But when I saw you were being hired as a website manager; I knew something had to be done. I couldn't stand the thought of you spending all your time in the development room when I could have you all to myself." I got up and joined her at the watercooler, taking the paper cup from her hand and refilling it for her.

She took it with a certain numbness.

"And if you really want to have a hand at our website, I won't stop you. But, first and foremost, you'll be working for me. You'll be accompanying me during meetings, scheduling my appointments, and taking my calls."

She pressed her lips together like she was about to say something, but instead she downed her second cup of water.

"I hope you do not mind. I figured this would be a good way for us to get to know each other and determine whether we're a good match for one another or whether I should be drawing up our divorce papers." I planted a hand on the wall behind her and pivoted my body so she was forced to step back – to look up at me with those doe eyes of hers.

"What are the odds?" she mumbled under her breath.

"I'd say, one in a million." My voice was a low whisper

as I brought my lips closer to hers. She arched her back ever so slightly and it was enough for me to know her desire. She wanted me just as much as I wanted her. How was I to get in the way of that? "Something keeps bringing us together, Poppy." I moved even closer, our faces merely inches apart. "Can't you see that this was meant to be this way?"

I heard her shuddering breath. Her eyes searched mine while her hands trembled, still holding the paper cup. "Mr. Baker said there would be added benefits..."

"Does this mean you're considering my offer?" I asked.

"I'm thinking about it."

"Perhaps I should sweeten the deal..." I left her at the watercooler and locked the door. The soft *click* seemed to echo with the possibilities. Now that I had her all to myself, I could let my fantasies run wild. "Yes," I said. "There are added benefits that come with being my personal assistant and I truly believe you'll enjoy them." Without another word, I took her by the wrist, positioning her right in front of my desk. "As you've said once before, I make it very difficult to say no." That's when I kissed her. I didn't hold back. For years, I had imagined fucking someone in my office and now, the time had finally come.

She brought the heat, her lips dancing the tango with mine. Our tongues joined in, tangling together and expressing the passion we both felt. That was the thing about Poppy – she never backed down. She was always ready for another round.

I grabbed her by the hips and lifted her off the ground. Her legs came around my waist, ankles locking behind my back as she grabbed at my hair. We were still making out, our lips locked together like we had fastened them with glue.

A small moan escaped her lips as I gave her ass a

squeeze. "You like that?" I breathed against the side of her neck.

"Mhm," was all she managed to say as she bit down on my earlobe and gave it a tug. She didn't stop there. Her teeth followed an invisible line down the side of my neck. All the while, she was working on the buttons of my shirt. It fell to the floor. She rested her hands on my bare chest, her eyes daring me to make the next move.

Be careful what you wish for, I thought as I swept the desk clean. It didn't matter to me that my expensive computer was now on the floor, probably broken. I could always buy another one. What mattered was getting Poppy in a bent-over position, ass in the air, and having my way with her.

I thought about tearing off the dress, but it simply looked too good to ruin. So, I hiked up her skirt revealing a pair of silken legs and an ass that was out of this world. It wasn't the first time I had seen it, but it was the first time I had seen Poppy wearing a thong. It was bright red and made of a lacey material. "I think someone came here with the intention of being a bad girl."

Smack!

She jumped but the wiggle of her hips told me that she had liked it – that she wanted more. Soon, her ass was bright red and radiating with heat. Still, she swung her hips from side to side trying to tempt me for more. Was there no satisfying this woman?

Smack!

This time, I did not remove my palm from her cheek. I kept it there, rubbing her skin for a moment, giving it time to recover.

In the window's newly cleaned surface, I could see our reflection. There was a look of pleasure on Poppy's face, but

I wanted more than that. I wanted to see her eyes rolling into the back of her skull and her lips parted with ecstasy-filled screams. Explaining the noise to Mr. Baker and his secretary would be something to deal with at a later time. Right now, all that mattered was getting to that wetness between her legs.

I tucked my thumb underneath the waistband of her thong and pulled it away from her skin. She clawed at the edge of my desk as the lace buried between her slit.

I pulled harder until I heard the *snap* of the material. I flicked it away and ran my hands along her ass once more. "Oops," I said. "Looks like you'll be leaving your panties behind."

13

POPPY

Things had taken an unexpected turn. One second, I was plagued by nerves thinking I would get rejected from the website manager position I had applied for and, in a way I had. Being Connor's personal assistant was not my career path of choice, but with equal pay and added *benefits,* how could I walk away?

I felt a breeze pass between my legs. Once again, Connor had ruined a perfectly good pair of panties and as a result, I would be returning home feeling the wetness slide down my legs. And, he knew it too – the sly devil.

His fingers tiptoed around my clit, not yet giving me what I wanted. I bit my bottom lip trying to curb the lust I felt building up in my core. If I didn't hold it back, I would explode at first touch and I didn't want that because a prolonged orgasm is so much better. Why do you think foreplay is so popular with the ladies?

"What's the matter?" he whispered against my ear. "Don't you want me?" His middle finger slipped between my lips, gliding along until it found my hole. He pressed inside. "I thought you would be wetter than this." His finger turned slowly like he was winding me up. "I thought you'd be *dripping* with excitement. Maybe we should try and fix that." Suddenly, a second finger came into play. Together, he pumped them in and out of my entrance, loosening it up for the main attraction that was still to come.

His thumb came around to my clit, as he flicked it back and forth. I bucked my hips, barely able to stand it, but he pressed his other hand down on the small of my back, keeping me pinned against his desk. With no hope of getting away, I was at his mercy, shaking in the wake of his touch. Connor knew what he was doing. He'd speed up just to slow down just as I was reaching the edge. He would draw slow circles around my clit with his thumb whenever he reached that crescendo just to keep me on the brink. He was testing my sanity and damn, I liked it.

"Fuck, Connor, you can't do this to me."

"Can't I?" Suddenly, he had me turned around, legs in the air. His pants were down around his ankles, cock out and ready. Roughly, he pulled me towards the edge and rammed right inside. I felt the scream in my throat before it ripped through the office, muffling the sound of his balls slapping against my skin, likely painting my ass an even darker shade of red.

He grabbed my breasts through my dress and kneaded them between his fingers as he continued his assault. Holding back was no longer an option. I was screaming his name by the time he threw my legs over his shoulders.

The position did something for the pleasure. It pulsated through every nerve in my body, sending me into yet another orgasm, and Connor seemed to have no intention of slowing down. His teeth were set and his eyes wild. He was getting closer and closer to climax. I could tell by the way his cock became rock hard inside me.

Abruptly, he stopped, pulling out and leaving me empty. I begged him to continue, but he was breathing hard, rocking on his heels. Had he already climaxed? Craning my neck, I could see no sign of a mess. I cocked my head in question and he answered by bending me over once again. This time around my legs were jelly, sapped of strength after the countless orgasms he had put me through. They had simply rolled one into the other until I could no longer keep track. Connor was good like that.

He placed his hands on my hips and pressed himself against me. His entire length was throbbing, ready to blow, but instead of taking me from behind like I expected him to, he simply ran his tip up and down my slip.

"Please..." I begged, surprising even myself because, after all the ecstasy, I still wanted more.

I could see his smirk in the window. He was the sexiest devil I had ever seen.

He pressed his tip into my waiting hole, but still, he held off. I tried to push myself into him, but he pulled back, his grimace deepening with my frustration. Connor was having too much fun with this little game of his and it was going to cost him. Maybe not today and maybe not tomorrow, but I was going to get him back for all this teasing.

His thumb returned to action, circling around and around.

"Please..." My voice was a high-pitched mewl.

His thumb picked up speed. Another orgasm ran through my spine leaving me breathless and that's when he slipped inside. His cock filled my every inch, pushing me to the breaking point. He eased himself down to the very base, settling there for a moment while he kissed the back of my neck and ran his fingers along my thighs, nice and gentle.

I sucked in a shuddering breath as he began to move, slow and steady. The fire burning between us smoldered, hotter than ever. This was even better than his animalistic thrusting because every push and pull was pronounced.

He grunted, doing everything he could just to keep going a little while longer. Every second felt like a minute when the sex was this good. I was holding onto the edge of the desk, my back arched, toes curled. "Fuck!" I screamed, not for the first time.

There was now a puddle on Connor's desk, but he didn't seem to mind. He was living for it, making each thrust just a little bit harder. Then, unexpectantly, he pulled my hair. I gasped and felt another wave of pleasure explode within me.

Seconds later, Connor followed suit. I could feel his stickiness all over my ass. Panting, he fell back, landing in one of the leather seats while I was left bent over, unable to move for my legs had gone from jelly to wet noodles.

After catching his breath, he grabbed a few tissues from the box on the floor and cleaned up his mess. "I think that's everything," he said, throwing yet another wad into the trash.

"Someone had a good time," I purred, finally able to stand despite the shaking in my legs. I wasn't sure whether I would be able to walk straight for the rest of the day.

"You?" He smirked and helped me to a seat. "So, is it safe to say that you'll be accepting my offer?"

"You're a very persuasive man, Mr. Dresden. In the last couple of days, you have gotten me to do things I never imagined myself doing. Of course, getting some action in a corporate office has always been a fantasy of mine, but I never thought I'd get the opportunity to act on that fantasy, let alone with my new boss." I took him by the chin and kissed him. I couldn't quite explain it but being with Connor made me feel adventurous. I was no longer concerned with repercussions because I was riding on instincts. It was one hell of a way to live and frankly, I think I preferred it.

14

CONNOR

"First order of business." I held up my laptop. The screen was shattered and displaying nothing but black. "Looks like I'll be needing another."

"Jeez, you really did a number on that thing, but I will admit, it was pretty sexy when you just swiped your desk clean in your eagerness to fuck me." She took me by the shirt and pulled me closer. "It felt like we were in a movie."

I held her and smiled. "Only this is better because it's real and we can do it whenever we want."

"What about Mr. Baker and his secretary? Won't they start asking questions? I mean, I wasn't exactly quiet. I wouldn't be surprised if the whole city had heard me scream your name."

"Let's keep it that way," I said as I grabbed her ass. Doing so reminded me of the fact that she no longer wore any panties. "Anyway, would you mind going down to the tech department and getting me another laptop. They should have a spare I can use until I order myself another one."

Her eyes widened. "You do realize that my panties are in your trash can, don't you?"

"I'm aware," I answered with a nonchalant tone. "If I were you, I'd be careful about bending over."

She glared but it did nothing to change my mind. In the end, she pulled down her dress skirt as far as it would go and walked out the door. I leaned back in my desk chair wondering what kind of looks she would get from Mr. Baker and his secretary. Stephanie, in particular, was probably sitting in a catatonic state, a permanent blush coloring her features. She was one of those religious types. I didn't mind it. She simply wasn't my type. If what I did with Poppy was sin, then send me straight to Hell.

***

WHEN POPPY RETURNED, there was lunch on the coffee table. "I thought you might want something to eat."

"Thanks." She examined her sandwich. "Turkey?"

"Hope you don't mind. I wasn't sure what you liked. I thought turkey would be a safe bet."

"Not my favorite but definitely serviceable."

"So, what is your favorite?"

"Deli meat?"

I nodded.

"Probably roast beef."

At these words, I handed her my sandwich. "Here. Take it. Roast beef happens to be my favorite as well."

"You're giving me your sandwich?" Poppy asked.

"Yes. I want you to enjoy your lunch. It is the least I can do after throwing you such a curveball. I know you had no intention of becoming my personal assistant, but I promise you, I'll make it worth your while."

"Oh, I believe you." Finally accepting the trade, she took a bite, her eyes lighting up as her taste buds rejoiced. *Oliver's Deli* made the best sandwiches in town, no doubt about it. A few years ago, I had tried to convince Oliver to franchise, but he insisted on keeping his original location. He was happy where he was and didn't want any additional headaches. I couldn't blame the guy, though as he got closer and closer to retirement age, I feared I would soon be without my go-to meal.

"Speaking of your new position, I have some paperwork from HR for you to fill out. Once that's taken care of, you'll officially be on the payroll."

"And I suppose it also means we're officially engaged."

Poppy was playing with her ring, her face hard to read. "I suppose it does. How does it feel?"

"Honestly?"

"Honestly," I said.

"It feels kind of strange. Every girl has a dream of finding Mr. Right and living out that happily ever after. This isn't exactly that. No offense, but I don't really know who you are. Jenna never bothered to tell me anything about you or your bother. All I really know is that you're one hell of a whirlwind in bed—"

"And out," I interrupted, glancing at the desk.

"And out," she agreed.

We finished our lunch and Poppy set to work filling out her paperwork. From my desk, I couldn't help peeking over at her from time to time. It was a nice change of pace to have someone else in the office. It helped take off the edge of loneliness that often found me while I was at work.

"Would you like a coffee?" I asked.

"No thanks. I'm more of a tea drinker."

"I have tea here as well, but I'll be honest, I don't quite know how to go about making it."

"You just steep the teabag in a mug of hot water for a couple of minutes." She joined me at the coffee machine and browsed through the selection I had to offer her. Standing so close to her, I picked up on the scent of her shampoo. It was something sweet, laced with hints of honey and maybe even a bit of mango. It drew me closer. Her arm brushed against mine and I felt a tingle of excitement underneath my skin. It wasn't a desire to have her again but something more – something deeper.

"See? Simple," she said as she dunked the teabag into some hot water. "And then you just add some milk and sugar, just like you would a coffee."

As she spoke, my phone went off. I took it out of my pocket and saw a calendar notification on the screen. "Shoot, I forgot."

"Oh?"

"I have a meeting with my personal trainer, Rhianna, this afternoon."

Poppy chuckled. "With a body like that, I should have known you were something of a gym rat."

Knowing it wouldn't bother her, I changed into my gym clothes right in front of her, enjoying her reaction a bit too much. The sparkle in her eye almost had me canceling the appointment, but if I wanted to continue rocking her world then I needed to keep myself in shape. "You are more than welcome to tag along."

"And workout in a dress? More than that, I don't think your gym would appreciate if I used their equipment being as wet as I am."

"You're still wet?" I asked, eyebrow raised with interest.

"Have you forgotten what you did to me?" To prove her

point, she brought my hand between her legs. True to her word, she was soaking wet. "Maybe next time," she said. "As for today, I'll see you at home." She paired her wink with a vixen smile. This girl was definitely something else. Getting a ring on her finger was nothing short of hitting the jackpot.

BY THE END of my training session, I was sweating bullets. Rhianna, my trainer, had me pushing the pace for the entire hour.

"Don't tell me you're tired," she said, throwing me a bottle of water. "Because there's more of this come tomorrow."

"I think you're trying to kill me."

"Hardly." Rhianna wiped the sweat from her brow. "Because if I manage to kill you with my training then I'm both without a client and a potential date."

"Excuse me?" I couldn't be sure whether I had heard her right. Rhianna had always been a tad bit flirty, but she had never been so bold.

"My cousin just invested in a night club and I was looking for a date to bring along to the grand opening. It's going to be a pretty sweet little shindig." She moved with confidence like a lioness about to make that fatal pounce. "And I would really love it if you could come along." There was a thick layer of sugar in her voice as she batted eyelashes. "I promise, you'll have one hell of a time."

It was then that I noticed we were alone in the locker room. Rhianna had noticed it, too. She stepped forward, trying to get me into the corner, but I stood my ground. No doubt, the uninterested expression on my face made her come to a stop. "I'm sorry, Rhianna, but I can't come with you."

"Why not?" she demanded. "I thought you liked night clubs."

"I do. That's not the problem."

Her confidence wavered.

"I'm engaged."

"Engaged," she spat. "To who? Last I knew, you weren't dating anyone. I checked your social media profile right before you arrived, and it said you were still single."

I shrugged. "I don't know what to tell you. I don't always update, but officially, I'm off the market."

She shook her head. "All I need is a minute to change your mind." Before I could stop her, she had me by the shirt. With one yank, our lips came crashing together. Her strength surprised me because for a few seconds there, I couldn't pull away. Her lips burned against mine, but it wasn't anything I enjoyed. Quite honestly, it felt *wrong*. All I could think about was Poppy and how she would react if she saw me kissing my personal trainer. Sure, our relationship was far from conventional but still, I felt unfaithful.

Managing to get my arms between us, I shoved Rhianna off of me. "Don't ever do that again."

15

POPPY

"Hello? Is this Charles?" I was holding the chauffeur's card in my hand. After Connor left for the gym, I stuck around a little while longer to finish up the paperwork he had tasked me with. I knew he probably wouldn't have minded if I left it for tomorrow, but I've always been a hard worker, sometimes to a fault.

"It is."

"This is Poppy."

"Who?"

"Pomona," I corrected. "Sorry, I usually go by Poppy. It's a bit less formal sounding."

"Ah, of course. What can I do for you, Poppy? Shall I pick you up from D & D?"

"If you wouldn't mind that would be great."

"Certainly."

"And there's one more thing. It's sort of a strange request but I really don't know who else to ask." I could feel my face becoming red hot. I poured some water from the watercooler but didn't drink it. "Would you mind bringing along a pair of my panties? They are in my luggage bag in the outside pocket. I'm really sorry about asking–"

"Say no more. I'll make sure it is seen to." Charles spoke with a tone of professionalism.

I breathed a sigh of relief for I had been expecting a very awkward conversation. Had he dared to ask what had happened to my original pair of panties, I really did not know what I would have told him.

"Do you know when you'll be here?"

"In about fifteen minutes or so."

"Perfect. I'll wait for you in the lobby."

On my way down, I had the misfortune of sharing an elevator with Mr. Baker. I could tell that he knew. I mean, my screams had probably made it pretty obvious what we were doing in Connor's office. As my face became the color of a ripened beet, I avoided looking him in the eye. It was hard to stand still – to keep my mouth shut – when I knew this man probably thought I was sleeping my way into the position. I was desperate to explain myself, but was the truth really any better?

In the end, we went our separate ways.

Stephanie, the secretary, quickened past me. She was as red with embarrassment as I was.

Charles came not a minute too soon for the AC was cranked up higher in the lobby than anywhere else in the building and it was getting a little uncomfortable to shoot the breeze. He handed over a brown paper bag. "I shall wait for you by the car. It is parked out front."

I nodded my thanks before dashing into the bathroom. *Ah, that feels much better,* I thought.

Charles opened the door to the backseat, but I did not jump inside.

"Would you mind if I rode in the front? It just feels

awfully weird being in the back and talking to you through the partition."

"Certainly." Charles could not mask the surprise from his face, but he did not argue with my request. "Where to?" he asked once he was behind the wheel. "To the manor or elsewhere?"

"When do you get off your shift?"

Again, his face was painted by surprise. "I work from one to eight."

"Okay, so if I make a little stop before going back to the manor, I won't be keeping you from your family?"

"You are very considerate," he commented.

"I try to be," I said. "You have been generous in helping me with my...predicament. The least I can do is treat you with fairness and respect."

Charles was looking at me like I was some sort of alien from a distant planet. "Many people do not think so." His voice became hushed. "I hope I can say this in confidence but many of Connor's guests have proved very entitled and I believe it is the reason they never remain for very long."

"Oh? What sort of guests?"

"I fear I have spoken out of turn." His attempt to retract the conversation gave it away. Charles was talking about Connor's previous girlfriends. At once, my mind started to wander. How many had there been? Had they been as stuck up as Charles said? And was that really the reason Connor broke up with them? Or was it something else entirely?

Charles cleared his throat and adjusted his hat in the mirror.

"So, where was it that you wanted to go?"

"Right." I smoothed the fabric of my dress against my legs just to distract myself from the awkwardness that had built up inside the cab of the car. "On the way here, I saw a pawn shop advertising rare books. I have something of a collection back in Atlanta and I would love to add to it once all my stuff gets shipped."

"Ah, *Ends and Oddities*. It is a lovely little shop. It would be my pleasure to bring you there."

The ride was short and passed in silence. I was almost glad to get out of the car. The fresh air helped clear my mind of Connor's past. What did it really matter? Their engagement was just an act and as long as he kept me employed and satisfied, who was I to complain?

And yet, there was a part of me that wanted more. I could pretend I was completely unattached and that feelings weren't part of the equation, but who was I kidding? With every smile, I felt myself becoming fonder. Why should I cross him off my list simply because our arrangement was unorthodox? Hell, if all worked out, it would make one hell of a story for the kids.

I stopped.

Am I really thinking about having kids with Connor?

I shook my head and tried to quell my imagination because obviously, it had ventured into uncharted territory. Luckily, *Ends and Oddities* had plenty in terms of distraction. The back wall was filled with books, floor to ceiling. I gravitated towards the shelf marked 'rare.' Picking a book at random, I pulled out a leather-bound book about Victorian hairstyles. The illustration embossed on the front was just downright ridiculous.

"It's a wonder how they managed to keep their hair in such precarious fashion." I turned around and was met with the sight of an older woman. She was a bit of an oddball herself with rings stacked on every finger and mismatched clothing brighter than a strobe light at a rave. "They had all kinds of techniques, some of them quite dangerous."

"Is that so?"

"Mmm." She pressed her lips together in what I took to be a strange sort of 'yes.' The bands on her wrist jangled as she reached for a book with a deep blue cover. "Now, if you're looking for something to add to your collection, let me suggest this one. It's written by an unknown author, but it's a lovely story about this foreigner who falls in love with a young man and they unite to convince the man's father that she deserves a place in the village. When the father refuses, the young man marries her just to give her someplace to call home. I've always thought it would make a lovely fairytale, but because the author is unknown, it has never been given much notice."

There was a strange similarity between the story and what was going on in my own life. "I'll take it."

"Splendid. Splendid. I knew you would." She brought it to the counter and wrapped it up with some newspaper. "I must ask you something."

"And what might that be?"

"I see that you're wearing a lovely dress. It suits you rather well, my dear. I can only hope that your partner will be taking you on a date this evening. Where might he be?"

It was a weird question, though the person asking it wasn't exactly normal. "He's at the gym."

"You did not join him?" The woman had eyes that knew too much. It felt like she had the ability to look right through me. It was giving me the creeps but since I had yet to pay for the book, I wasn't about to walk away.

"He's with a personal trainer."

"Might her name be Rihanna?"

Goosebumps covered both my arms. "How did you know that?"

"My son dated a personal trainer once. I hope it is not the same woman, as she is nothing but a maneater. She's only after one thing and thankfully, I was able to knock some sense into my boy before she could fully sink her claws into his assets."

"Uh..." I didn't know what to say. "I can't say I'm very familiar with his personal trainer."

"You'd be wise to find out. Women like that will stop at nothing to get what they want. It will not matter whether they are with someone or not." I felt like I was at a fortune teller's booth and this woman was trying to keep me off some dark path.

"Right." I rummaged through my purse, looking for my wallet. "So, how much for the book?" The woman's intentions were probably good, but she was giving me this eerie feeling and I did not like it one bit. First, it was the book and then her son just so happened to have dated Connor's personal trainer.

"It's on the house. I only ask that you come again," she said with a smile.

"I will," I answered, not really thinking of the promise I was making.

"Have a splendid evening," she called out with a wave as I made my way out the door.

"That was weird..." I whispered to myself once I was back inside the car.

"You mean Odette?" asked the driver.

"What?"

"The owner of the pawnshop. Her name is Odette and true to her name, she can be a little strange. She used to be a soothsayer before she decided to open this little shop with all the trinkets she's collected over the years. A good woman, really, so long as you can get past her mannerisms."

I turned in his direction. "Did you say she was a soothsayer? Like someone who can see the future?"

"That's what she used to claim." Charles shrugged. "If you ask me, it's just a bunch of fancy guesswork, nothing more. But if you believe in that sort of stuff, I am sure Odette would be happy to indulge you."

"I think I'll pass," I said, remembering the eerie feeling the woman had left her with.

"Very well. Is there anywhere else you'd like to go, or shall I take you home?"

"Home. Please." I leaned my head back and closed my eyes. I wanted to forget what Odette had told me about Connor's trainer, but it had infected my mind. If this Rhianna person was as easy to put out as Odette had suggested, why hadn't Connor asked her to participate in the fake marriage thing first? Clearly, he knew her, probably trusted her, so why hadn't he slipped a ring on her finger and asked her to play along? It had to mean something but what exactly?

The countless questions made my head spin. I pushed them aside, distracting myself by opening my purchase for the very first time. The pages crinkled, showing their age, but they were in good condition despite being of another century.

"Get anything good?" Charles asked. He was a bit chattier now that we sat side by side. I really didn't mind it. The chauffeur was an easy person to talk to.

"Odette recommended it." I ran my finger along the spine. The title, once written in gold lettering had faded away leaving nothing but a few vague outlines. "It's something of a fairytale. Honestly, it isn't something I would usually read, but Odette made it sound like one hell of a story and I just couldn't leave it behind."

"She has a way of doing that. How do you think she stays in business? She's one hell of a saleswoman."

I agreed with him and started reading the first couple of pages. It was written in that fairytale language, but the narrator was different – omniscient in a sarcastic sort of way like he was keeping some great big secret from me. Effortlessly, I was reeling into the world of this couple, cheering for their success from the start.

"We're here," announced Charles.

Finding it hard to put the book down, I read until the end of the page before finally prying myself away. "Sorry."

"Looks like you've found yourself a good book."

"I think I have." With the book tucked under my arm, I headed for the front door. It was opened by a member of staff before I could even knock.

Inside, I found Connor working on the couch, a new laptop perched on his lap. He was fresh out of the shower, his hair still wet. The scent of his body wash filled the entire room.

"Hey." He greeted me with a smile. It was the sort of smile I would expect a husband to use with his wife after a long day. "I didn't expect to get home first. Where did you go if you don't mind me asking?"

"*Ends and Oddities*," I said as I took a seat beside him. "I saw that they were selling old and rare books, so I thought I would check it out on the way home." It was difficult to keep from asking about Rhianna, but I didn't want to come across as being paranoid. Fake engagement or not, I owed Connor some extension of trust. Who was I accuse him when I knew next to nothing about his relationship with Rhianna? Besides, the agreement between us was a simple exchange. I'd help him convince his grandfather and should I succeed, I get to live rent-free. No talk of feelings and exclusivity had been expressed.

"Ah." Connor nodded knowingly. "So, you had a run-in with Odette?"

"I did."

"She's something of a local celebrity around here. You should have seen her when she was giving out fortunes. If you questioned her fashion sense today, you should have seen her then. She was like a walking circus tent." Glancing over at his screen, I saw him going through his email. There was no evidence he was talking to Rhianna outside of the gym. "But I have to admit, her fortunes were always scary accurate."

"Really?"

"No, of course not." He closed his laptop and held out the hand, asking to see the book. "What did Odette get you to buy?"

"I can't make out the title and the author is unknown, but from what she told me, it's something of a fairytale about star-crossed lovers. I wasn't going to buy it, but as you must know, Odette is quite the saleswoman."

"So, if not this, what were you intending to buy?"

"There was a book there on Victorian hairstyles – a manual of sorts." I dropped my eyes, suddenly bashful about sharing my passion.

"Oh?"

Despite the heat rising through my cheeks, I felt a need to tell Connor about my love for hair. "You see, at one point I thought about being a hairdresser. I went through beauty school and everything, but the bills weren't getting paid and no one cared to hire someone with little to no experience. So, I took to designing websites as a freelancer. It paid well

– paid for my degree, in fact. And that's how I came to apply for the web manager position at your company."

Connor looked impressed, which filled me with a sort of pride. "That's quite the story. I have to admire you for sacrificing your dream of being a hairdresser for the sake of being responsible. It isn't something most people would do. They'd rather remain a starving artist."

"I miss it. I do. But it is what it is."

"You know my grandmother runs a chain of hair salons. It's a small operation but she does it more as a passion project than anything else. She's pushing eighty and still cutting hair. My grandfather refuses to let anyone else approach him with clippers."

"Your grandparents sound sweet."

"They are. I was lucky enough to be raised by their hand." I felt a thread of Connor's past at my fingertips. I thought about unraveling it. There were a million questions I could have asked him, but I decided to settle into the silence and hope that one day he would feel comfortable telling me everything there was to know about Connor Dresden.

16

CONNOR

The following day, I waited for Poppy in the kitchen with a cup of coffee and the day's paper. The stock market was looking pretty good, but it could be better. I made a mental note to get in touch with my investor just to make sure things were sound because when it came time for my retirement, I had every intention of never lifting a finger.

These thoughts were usually ones of me sipping cocktails by the beach, but suddenly there was someone else alongside me.

Poppy.

She had made her way into my future and I've got to say, she looked pretty good there. I wondered whether it could really happen. Could we really grow old together? Was there enough chemistry outside of the bedroom to make it work?

Before I could make my conclusion, Poppy walked into the kitchen wearing a simple summer dress and a neutral-colored cardigan over her shoulders. "I'm going to have to go shopping soon," she said.

"That can be arranged," I said. There was really

nothing provocative about her outfit. It was really quite modest, but still, I felt my attraction mounting as she joined me at the table. It was a need to be next to her – to hold her. "And what about your things in Atlanta? Aren't you having them shipped here?"

"That's the plan. I'll have to talk to my old roommate and see if she won't box everything up for me." She drenched her French toast in syrup before cutting it into bite-sized pieces. I found myself drawn to every movement she made. There was a sort of mysticism about this woman that I had never seen in another. Odette would have called it a connection of the souls and maybe it was, but from a pragmatic perspective, I knew it was still too soon to tell.

I finished my coffee and folded my newspaper, putting it aside so I could better focus on the gorgeous woman sitting across from me. "I was thinking we could share a ride to work. There's no need to bother a chauffeur if we're both going the same way."

"So, are you driving, then?" she asked.

"I am. Why? Is that a problem?"

"Not at all. I just assumed that maybe you didn't have a license or something."

I laughed. "I got my permit as soon as I was fifteen and a half. I skipped school that day and everything."

"And your grandparents allowed that?"

"It took a bit to convince my grandmother, but it had been my grandfather's idea. He loves cars and wanted to see me behind the wheel as soon as possible. You know, he picked up my grandmother at a drive-in. She worked the concession stand and he would watch a movie every day just to see her. Back then, he didn't have a cent to his name, but she fell in love with his charm. The rest is history." I stole an apple tart from Poppy's plate before getting up and grabbing my keys. "Shall we?"

"Isn't it a little early? I thought we started at nine."

"We do."

"So, why are we leaving now?"

"Because there's somewhere I want to go before we head into the office," I said.

I took her by the hand and pulled her up. Forgetting how small she was, I pulled a little too hard and her body crashed into mine. I steadied her by wrapping my arms around her waist, holding close. Time seemed to stop as I looked down and fell into the depth of her eyes. Without thinking, I kissed her. It was the most natural thing in the world.

We were both smiling when we finally pulled away from one another. Wanting the blissful moment to last, I placed my hand in hers and brought her into the garage.

She stopped at the door like her feet had suddenly become glued to the floor.

"What's wrong?" I asked.

"Do all of these cars belong to you?"

"Every last one," I said. "My grandfather isn't the only one who loves cars. I guess you could say I inherited that from him."

"This is quite the...collection." I saw her eyes gravitating towards a baby blue model. It happened to be one of my favorites and the one I was taking out that very morning. It would seem great minds think alike. "How much does something like this cost?" she asked as she ran her finger along the chrome detailing.

"Why, are you thinking about getting one for yourself?" I opened the door for her and helped her inside.

"If I had the cash and I knew how to drive, I totally

would." She buckled herself in as I started the car. It was always a joy to hear the motor purring under the hood. "Maybe you could help teach me?"

"I'd love to," I said, and it wasn't a lie. I was a very busy man and more often than not, my schedule was jammed packed, but it didn't feel like a burden to take time out of my day to help Poppy. It felt *right*.

My hand rested on the shifter as I made my way toward the city. Poppy found it, squeezing it gently just to tell me she was there.

I could get used to this, I thought.

"You still haven't told me where we're going."

"To see Odette."

"Odette?" Poppy questioned. "Isn't it a little too early for a fortune-telling?"

"We're not going there to get our fortunes read."

"Then why else? I can't say I think of you as a thrifter."

"We're going to get that book on Victorian hairstyles. I want you to have it." This time, I was the one squeezing her hand.

"You really didn't have to drive all the way out here for my sake."

"If it'll make you happy, then it'll be worth it." I brought her fingertips to my lips, kissing them with a tenderness that came straight from the heart.

There was another car parked in front of the pawnshop. It looked familiar, but I couldn't think of who owned the black sedan. The license plate didn't help to ring any bells. Figuring I would find out who it was soon enough, I stopped wracking my brain and rounded the front of the car. I didn't get to Poppy's door fast enough for she was already getting out. I held out my hand and she took it.

What felt like a zap of electricity coursed through my

veins, accelerating the beating of my heart. What was it about this girl that made me feel so *alive?*

Hand in hand, we walked into the store. To my surprise, Rhianna was standing at the counter holding what appeared to be a diamond bracelet. "It has to be worth more than that," she said, her tone curt. "He told me it was genuine."

Odette humored her customer and considered the piece of jewelry under her jeweler's loop. "I'm sorry but this is cubic zirconia. I can give you twenty dollars for it and I'm really being quite generous with you despite your misgivings with my son."

Rhianna huffed. "Your son was a joke. Now, I say you quit playing me and give me the real value of this bracelet because I'm not letting you have it for twenty dollars."

Poppy slipped out of my grasp and marched right up to Rhianna. "You've got some kind of nerve," she said, standing tall. Oh, she meant business. I almost felt sorry for Rhianna because she was about to get the beat down of the year. "Where do you get off insulting this woman? It isn't her fault that your boyfriend gave you fake diamonds. You should just be happy he got you anything at all. Maybe a $20 bracelet is all he could afford." With every word, her tone became icier.

"Who the hell are you to give me a lecture? I don't see a halo on your head. Don't kid yourself, sweetheart, you aren't a saint so stop acting like one." She snatched up her bracelet. "You won't be getting any of my future business."

Odette smiled. "I would say that it's been a pleasure but that would be a lie."

Rhianna huffed and was about to storm out the door when she spotted me standing nearby. In an instant, her scowl was replaced by bedroom eyes. Her bottom lip jutted out ever so slightly in what I had to guess was her attempt at a sexy pout. "Oh, Connor, I didn't see you there." She stretched out every syllable like she was about to sing a song. "You aren't here with *her*, are you?" She pointed her thumb at Poppy. "Did you see how she came up to me barking like a mad bitch. The nerve of some people."

My blood boiled to hear her insult Poppy right to my face.

"And I've been meaning to call you and ask whether you changed your mind about my invitation. Maybe I was a little forward at the gym, but I thought you'd agree once you knew what you were missing out on."

"Frankly, I'm not missing out on much," I said, my tone steady. Keeping one's temper always packs a bigger punch. It has a way of getting under an opponent's skin.

"What?"

"You heard me. I wasn't interested then and I'm not interested now." I added insult to injury by wrapping my arm around Poppy's shoulder. "I've found myself someone amazing."

She sized up Poppy for a moment, looking like she was a contender in a cage match. I stepped in front of my fiancée, holding out my arm as a sort of shield. It wasn't that I thought Poppy would lose in a fight. In fact, if I had to bet on it, I would put all my money on Poppy. She was the fiercer of the two, but I just didn't want to see her stoop down to Rhianna's level.

"You're delusional if you think she has anything on me."

"And you're delusional to think I would ever give a gold digger such as yourself a chance. You might as well wait for Hell to freeze over."

At this, Odette chimed it. "The stars predict such an event happening in approximately 2.3 billion years."

"Hear that? You can try being my girlfriend in 2.3 billion years. Until then, you might want to start looking for a new client because I'd rather be out of shape than have to train alongside someone who treats people like shit."

Rhianna stood there clutching the strap to her designer bag until the tips of her fingers went a bright shade of white. By contrast, her face went a deep shade of crimson and growing darker by the second. Clearly, I had struck a nerve. Good. With an attitude like hers, she needed to be taught a lesson.

"Good day," I said with a nod of my head.

With nothing to say, she huffed and turned on her heels. Through the window I watched her throw the bracelet to the ground and stomp on it. For someone who had been so adamant about having something of value, she was quick to throw it away. Of course, it had been a con. Women like Rhianna only want one thing.

"So, that was your personal trainer?" Poppy asked once I rejoined her at the counter. Odette had disappeared.

"Yeah, was," I said. "She's one hell of a trainer, but she won't see me stepping foot into her gym ever again. I'm not about to shell out money to someone who treats others like bugs beneath her feet."

"Good." Poppy looked around. "Any idea where Odette went? She just sort of vanished."

"She'll turn up," I said. "She always does."

"So, you had no idea she was like that?"

"Who? Rhianna?"

Poppy nodded.

"Honestly, for the most part, I'm too winded during our training sessions to bother with conversation. Only recently has she shown interest in me outside the gym."

"Oh?" Something flashed behind Poppy's eyes. Was she

jealous? I searched her face, looking for answers, but she dropped her gaze to the display case beside us. There were some unusual trinkets, though none of them held my attention now that there was a chance Poppy was legitimately interested in me.

"She asked me to accompany her to the grand opening of this club her cousin recently bought. Now that I think about it, I think she just recently broke up with her boyfriend. He was a stockbroker, I think."

"Aha." Poppy nodded knowingly. "She needed someone else to supply the gifts." She threw back her head and laughed. "But the joke's on her because this guy was smart enough to get her the cheap stuff."

I laughed alongside her before she stopped and looked at me with a stare so intense, it stopped the world from spinning. "Would you ever date someone like that? I mean if she was smoking hot and lacked a thread of decent moral fiber?"

"That isn't a question," I said. "Of course, I would want to date a beautiful woman. I would be lying if I said looks weren't at least part of the equation but they aren't everything. I want more than a girlfriend. I want a *partner,* and for someone to be my partner they have to be smart and funny and generous and kind." I was describing Poppy and everything about her that made my pulse quicken. "I want someone I can grow old with and share a thousand happy memories with."

Poppy looked like she was about to say something, but then all of a sudden, Odette appeared. "Here is that book you wanted."

"I didn't say I wanted a book," said Poppy, and yet, the book in Odette's hand was exactly what we had come to buy.

"We'll take it."

"How did she...?" Poppy scratched the side of her head. "I really didn't tell her we were here for the Victorian hair-style book."

"You expressed interest in it yesterday. I simply assumed you were here to see if it was still on my shelves. Often, when we leave things behind we return to find them again."

"There's something otherworldly about that woman," said Poppy once we were back in the car. "You have to agree that was pretty weird."

"She just has a good memory. I wouldn't worry too much about it." I tapped the cover of the book. "And I expect you to start wearing your hair like this or I'm going to have to call off this wedding."

"You better be careful what you wish for." Her carefree laugh filled the car and every chamber of my heart. Oh, if only I could hear that laugh for the rest of my days.

17

POPPY

It was a *good* morning if you know what I mean. A few weeks into the job as Connor's personal assistant and I was really starting to dig the added 'benefits.' Despite having a room of my own, most nights were spent in my boss's bed because who wants to sleep alone if they could help it? And my usual insomnia wasn't so bad when there was someone to share my thoughts with. People often make a big deal of 'pillow talk' and I hadn't the slightest idea why, but it was extremely comforting to know I could turn over and have someone listen to me. We'd talk deep into the night about this or that. Sometimes we'd chase conspiracy theories or try to unravel a film we had watched earlier that night. But what I enjoyed the most was learning about the business – what he did as a kid – how he got a start in the world – everything. And he seemed just as interested in my story.

Wearing nothing but a silk robe, I went into the kitchen. Since it was a Saturday, most of the house staff had the day off, including the morning cook. It was always a little weird to hear the pitter-patter of my feet against the tile floor when usually the massive room was filled with the sounds of sizzling bacon or the whirling of a blender. Looking to fill the silence, I turned on the mansion's sound system. It started playing some smooth jazz. I bobbed my head with the beat as I made my way to the coffee machine. It was a fancy contraption with buttons enough to rival the cockpit of a plane.

I pressed what I hoped was the right combination of buttons for an espresso and crossed my fingers. The machine started sucking up water from the reserve so, clearly, something was happening. Then came the grind of coffee beans. I took a few steps away from the machine, always half afraid it would explode, but in the end, I was left with a steaming mug of coffee. Success! Pleased with myself, I carried the mug through the maze of halls looking for Connor. If I had to bet on it, he was probably tucked away in his home office. The guy had no concept of 'weekend.' He was a workaholic by every definition of the word, but I had to respect his work ethic for it had gotten him to where he was now. One does not become the CEO of a multi-million dollar corporation with satisfactory work alone.

Lo and behold, there he was sitting behind his desk. "I made you some coffee," I said. "Do you know what you want for breakfast?"

"Have one of the cooks make me a sandwich."

"It's Saturday, Connor. No one is here." I sat down on the edge of his desk, teasing him a bit by letting my robe fall open. Too focused on what was on his computer screen, he barely noticed. "Connor," I whispered, letting my voice take on a husky quality. Most nights he found it irresistible. A few naughty words were always enough to get us tangled under the sheets. He looked up, his eyes catching mine like a couple of magnets coming together. My heart swelled, becoming too big for my ribcage. It wasn't the first time it had reacted in such a manner. More and more often my pulse became erratic just at the sight of my fake fiancé.

"Right," he said, snapping back to reality. "We could grab a bite to eat. There's a nice diner in town with a really cozy vibe. I think you would like it there."

"Sounds nice," I said. "What are you working on anyway?"

"Just finished looking over a contract. I pay these lawyers all this money and in the end, I'm always the one making final revisions."

"Well, you *are* the boss." As I spoke those words, I grabbed him by the shirt and pulled him close enough where our lips were just about to touch. I smiled. "Now drink your coffee before it gets cold." I released my grip and leaned back. His features sharpened as he tried to keep the disappointment from his face.

"Yes, ma'am," he answered.

While he savored that first sip of coffee, I updated his word of the day calendar. "Malfeasance," I said. "A noun. Misbehavior; wrongdoing; illegal; unethical, or immoral conduct."

Connor smiled through his eyes, irises bright as he listened to me. "What you do to me is pretty malfeasance."

"I would say the same about what you do to me, but I don't believe you're using the word as a noun."

"Of course I am," he said. We bickered back and forth about who was right. It felt like we were an old married couple and that this sort of teasing was just a normal part of our morning routine.

"Hey!" I shouted in protest. "Kissing me won't make you right–" He silenced me with his lips. Soon, I was pressed against his bookcase, heart beating fast, leg around his waist. My tongue was about to meet his when he pulled away, leaving me grasping at thin air. Sometimes, payback is a real bitch.

"Oh, I've been meaning to ask you something," he said, acting as if nothing had happened. Nonchalantly, he picked up his mug and held it in both hands waiting for me to comment.

"And what might that be?"

"I have two tickets to a play. Would you like to come? There will be a surprise for whomever takes the second ticket and I would like very much for that someone to be you." He pulled the tickets from his top drawer and held them out for me to see.

"If not me, who else were you planning to take?"

"Oh, I don't know. Hugo, perhaps?"

"The gardener?" I laughed at the thought of the middle-aged man wearing anything but a Hawaiian shirt. "You sure you want to be seen with someone who wears galoshes on a daily basis? Rumor might spread that you're keeping the wrong company." I slide my finger along the edge of the tickets. They were beautiful, outlined in an intricate design of gold foil. The title of the play was written in a flowing script, simple yet elegant. "You know, I've always wanted to see this. Don't tell anyone but I'm something of a theater nerd; although, I've never been to a real fancy playhouse. All my friends were too lame to appreciate such things."

"Now's your chance," he said. "I have no problem being a theater nerd alongside you. But I have a request to make in return. I used to be part of a ballroom dancing group in college and I really miss it. Would you consider being my partner?"

"But I don't know how to ballroom dance."

"I'll teach you," he whispered. "Besides, you have it easy as a girl; all you have to do is follow me." He took me by the waist and guided me through the motions. "I think it would be a lot of fun and a fantastic thing for us to do together. Plus, I wouldn't mind spending some more time with you." His smile disarmed me, leaving me without a bone in my body. I fell limp against him. He held me even tighter, breath against my neck.

"Okay," I said. "Sign me up."

———

"MY BROTHER WILL BE HERE at any moment. He just called to say he was dropping by. I don't know what he wants, but I think it will be a good time to make introductions."

I gave him a playful pout. "So, you're telling me that I have to wear something other than this robe?"

"As much as it pains me to say so, yes. I don't want my twin getting any ideas."

I turned toward the door, but before I could move, Connor grabbed me by the wrist. The kiss that followed was one that took my breath away. He didn't say a word as he let me go. Walking in a daze, I managed to find my room, a smile plastered on my face. How was it that a fake relationship was making me so happy – giddy even?

In my room, I opened up the closet. Since receiving my first paycheck, I had stocked up on the essentials. My second and third paycheck were spent on other luxuries. The boutique stores were stocked with silken dresses and designer shoes. I had been tempted to overindulge, but I limited myself to one killer outfit. It was this outfit I laid out on the bed. It was a bit flashy to wear for a meet and greet, but I figured I would kill two birds with one stone and get ready for the play as well. Call me overeager, but I really wanted to know what Connor had in store for our date.

While I was doing my hair and makeup, I watched a bit of TV on my phone because curling a whole set of hair can prove quite boring when staring at a wall. With the help of some clips, I pinned part of my hair, going for that 20s vibe. It was only appropriate given the play we were attending.

Finished, I returned to Connor's office, expecting to find him there. What I didn't expect to find was his personal trainer. What was worse was the fact that she was sitting on his lap sucking face.

The words were taken right out of my mouth. All I could do was stare from the door while my heart broke into pieces. What was going on? Connor had made it clear that he would never waste his time with someone so poor of character. He had canceled every single one of his appointments and now, all of a sudden, she was in his office trying to score a run. Blinking, I felt the tears in my eyes. I wiped them away with the sleeve of my dress, angry with myself. Why had I been fool enough to believe him? Rhianna had the body of a goddess, toned and lean. Her skin was sun-kissed and perfect.

Unable to stand the sight of them any longer, I tore down the hall. I was out the door a moment later, my high heels turning precariously as I sped down the cobblestone driveway. I yanked them off my feet and continued barefoot down the road. It really did not matter to me where I went so long as I was far, far away from that damned mansion. Oh, why did I ever think it would work? Anyone with common sense would have suspected him from the start. After all, it just wasn't normal for a man to propose to a complete stranger. More than that, his reason for getting married wasn't a matter of love or spending the rest of his life with someone. It was a means to an end. I should have seen through his act – all his sweet moments – and seen him for what he really was – a villain with a plan.

I swore just to get some tension off my chest, but it barely helped. The image of Connor and Rhianna in that desk chair had been burned into my mind and I wasn't sure whether I would ever be free of it because I had allowed myself to fall and now I was paying the price for my mistake.

By the time I reached the city, it was starting to get dark and my feet were hurting. I needed a place to sit down. Spotting a bar, I made a b-line in its direction thinking that a drink might help clear things up. Maybe there was some-thing I was missing...

"What will it be?" The bartender was a friendly face.

"Something strong," I said, throwing my shoes on the floor. Getting the job as Connor's personal assistant felt like a step up in the world. I was making more than most web managers. It was the first time in my life where I was actu-ally able to afford something name brand. And for what? To be used. I was sick to my stomach. What was I supposed to do? I had declined my lease in favor of living at the mansion. Finding another would prove a nightmare and if I left D & D, how was I supposed to pay rent?

"You alright?" It was a familiar voice.

"Ryan?" I was surprised to see him. What were the odds? "What are you doing here?"

"I could ask the same of you. That dress is a bit overkill for a place like this." He rubbed the back of his neck real-izing what he had said. "Don't get me wrong, it looks lovely on you, but I can't help but think you were supposed to be somewhere else tonight."

"As a matter of fact, I was. But there's been a change of plans."

"Maybe a couple of rounds of pool will help get your mind off of whatever is bothering you," he suggested. "I know it always helps me."

"I've never played before."

"Don't worry. It's easier than it looks. I can show you." Before I could agree or disagree, he took my hand. I followed him, leaving my shoes and drinks behind.

From a wall, he picked out a pool stick and checked whether it was straight by holding it out and squinting with one eye closed. He looked ridiculous. I almost smiled, glad to focus on something other than the haunting image inside my head. "What was wrong with that one?"

"You'll never make a good shot with that piece of junk." He shook his head and grabbed another. "That's the problem with in-house sticks. They're all crap. Most people learn their lesson pretty quickly and bring their own."

"Did you?"

"Of course." He grabbed it and gave it a spin for dramatic effect. It was made of a glossy material, black all the way through with streaks of gold.

"I like the marble effect," I said. "Classy."

"Thanks. It cost me a pretty penny, but it was worth the investment. I've won a few tournaments with this baby so she's more than paid for herself."

"Tournaments, huh? You must be pretty good if you're winning competitions."

"I'm not one to brag, but I guess you could say I'm decent." He was racking up the balls. I picked up his pool stick and tried to figure out how to hold it, but it felt awkward in my hand. "Like this," he said, coming up from behind. His body was pressed against mine as he adjusted my grip. I thought he'd step aside, but he remained locked against me as he pulled back on my elbow, helping me make my first shot. The balls didn't scatter very far, though he praised my efforts all the same. He was just being nice. "Now, let a professional show you how it's done."

"So much for modesty."

He chuckled and rounded the table. I had no idea what he was aiming for, but in the blink of an eye, two solid-colored balls disappeared into opposite pockets. He sunk nearly every ball in his first move until he slipped up and missed completely. If you ask me, he did it on purpose.

"Way to give me a fighting chance," I said, taking the pool stick from his hand. Accidently, his fingers brushed mine. He stopped like he had been struck by Zeus' bolt. "Ryan?"

He shook his head. "Sorry."

Ryan made it obvious. He was the kind of person to wear his heart on his sleeve. This game of pool was his attempt at flirting, but I couldn't feel a thing. There wasn't that static in the air. My heart was beating at a steady pace. Ryan did nothing to fuel the fire in my stomach.

He wasn't Connor and never would be.

But he made a lot more sense. He was just a normal guy trying to score a girl. He didn't have an agenda.

"Do you want anything from the bar?"

"My pool skills making you nervous?" I asked, trying to lace a bit of playfulness into my voice. Sure, Connor had broken my heart, but I was strong enough to hold my head high and move on with my life. If he wanted to suck face with an arrogant bitch of a personal trainer then that was his prerogative.

"Definitely."

"A Coke," I said.

"Just a Coke?" he asked. "Are you sure?"

"Positive. Although, maybe with some ice."

"You got it." As he disappeared, I took off my engagement ring and threw it into my purse. If Connor wanted someone else, what was stopping me from doing the same?

18

CONNOR

"What the hell are you doing?" I returned to my office to find Neil sitting at my desk with his new girl-friend straddled across his lap. "I thought I told you to wait for me in the living room. I don't want you in here."

Neil flashed a schoolboy grin. "What's wrong? Don't want me knowing what you're doing in that fancy company of yours? Give it a break and get off your throne, will you? You've always acted like you were king of the castle, but we both know Gramps helped build your fortune."

"Sure, Gramps helped me. I won't deny that, but I actu-ally worked hard to get where I am now."

Neil scoffed. "Keep telling yourself that." He grabbed my ex-trainer and pulled her close. "Rhianna here was telling me that you found yourself a girl. That's news to me. I thought you would have at least told your dear old brother if you were serious enough to marry someone. I thought I would have seen her around, but this chick just popped up out of the blue. What are you playing at, Connor? How much are you paying her? And she could be the best damn actress in the world, but Gramps isn't going to fall for it, and you know it."

He had crossed the room, leaving Rhianna by the window. We squared off, shoulder to shoulder. I kept his gaze, standing firm.

That was the thing about my brother. He liked to act the playboy because it got him through the easy route in life; however, under the mask was someone truly cunning. He had proven himself manipulating and calculating. "So, where is she?"

"She should be down in just a minute."

Rhianna laughed, looking truly amused. "She's not worth your time, Neil."

"And where do you get off going after my brother?"

Neil stepped forward, holding out his arm to stop me from approaching. "You had your chance. It isn't my fault you decided to pass on the ass of the year. Really, it's quite the loss on your part."

"You don't know what you're getting yourself into," I said, even though I knew I was wasting my breath. They were made for each other.

Neil turned and stood by the globe, spinning it carelessly. Of course, he didn't care that he was playing with a priceless piece of history – it wasn't his. As a boy, Neil had done nothing but break my toys. Back then, I had been unable to do anything about it. Now that we were men, I wasn't one to let him push me around. I grabbed his wrist, my grip a bit too tight. He jerked it away. "Get out of my office," I said, my voice ice cold.

"Our grandparents would be very saddened to see you treating me with such rudeness. They raised us better."

"You're one to talk," I snapped. "Gramps worked hard

all his life. He tried to teach us the value of earning one's pay and yet you were slacking off at every opportunity and I was dumb enough to cover for you. Not anymore. If you want to go around acting like an entitled brat, I can't stop you, but I'm not going to encourage your laziness."

"Why do you think so poorly of me, Connor? What did I ever do to you?" He spoke like he was the most innocent man on the planet, despite being aware of our differences. This was just another way for him to get underneath my skin.

"Get out," I said again, quickly losing my patience. "I don't even want you to meet Poppy."

"Poppy? Is that her name? Quirky. I kind of like it." He retreated further into the room just to spite me. As he went, he took the liberty of touching everything within his reach. He even knocked some items to the ground.

"Will you ever stop acting like a child?" I accused. "We aren't kids anymore, Neil."

"When will you stop being so full of yourself? Smile sometimes, won't you?" He chortled and whisked Rhianna into his arms, dancing across the hardwood floor. My patience was being tested. I had the overwhelming urge to throw something at his face. If it wasn't obvious already, my brother and I weren't the twins that saw eye to eye. Every visit ended up like this. There was too much resentment between us – too many years of butting heads.

"I'm starting to think that this fiancée of yours isn't going to show. Maybe she saw how much of a bore you were and decided to leave you high and dry. It wouldn't be the first time, would it?" He pointed at the security cameras mounted in the corners of the room. "What was the name of the girl who pushed you to install those things? How many months did it take you to recuperate the money she'd stolen?" His laugh was like a jackhammer in my head. I couldn't stand it.

"Out!" I bellowed. "Or else I call security."

"You'd call security on your brother?" When I answered him with a stare, he held up his hands. "Alright, alright. I can take a hint." He took Rhianna by the hand and dragged her out the door. She giggled and shot me a look over her shoulder as if to say, '*look what you've been missing.*'

Too angry to follow them, I waited for the sound of the front door closing behind them. The home security app on my phone confirmed them leaving in Neil's sportscar. Seeing it made my blood boil by another ten degrees because I knew he had swindled that car from somebody else. He was just that kind of person – getting by on the backs of others. Sometimes, it made me sick to call him my brother. We really couldn't be any different.

Glad Poppy had missed meeting my brother, I went up to her room, expecting to find her there. She wasn't. She wasn't in the bathroom, either. I checked my bedroom, but it was empty, just like the rest of the house. Where could she have gone off to?

I checked the security footage and saw her leaving just shortly after my brother's arrival. She left in a rush almost like she was trying to get away from something. Taking a closer look at the video, I saw that she had been crying. "What happened?" I asked aloud, rewinding in an effort to find my answer. Five minutes before storming out, she had stood before the door for an awfully long time. The look on her face was that of someone who had just seen a ghost.

Switching cameras, I checked what was going on in the office at that time and of course, Neil was the culprit. He was making out with his girlfriend and from Poppy's perspective, it probably looked like I was the one making a move on the personal trainer. If only he had stayed out of my office like I had asked him to.

Okay, so Poppy thinks I'm a jackass. She probably hates me and thinks I'm some kind of douchebag who can't be trusted, but so long as I show her the footage, she'll believe me. Right? I mean, I can't possibly be in two places at once. And once she knows it was all just a misunderstanding, she'll come home where she belongs. I paced the front foyer, thoughts racing through my head.

Knowing I had to get in touch with Poppy, I called her number, but she didn't answer. I tried a second time with similar results. The third call went straight to voicemail.

AFTER DRIVING THROUGH TOWN, I was starting to get worried. Wherever she had gone, she was keeping herself out of sight. Even if I checked every establishment in town, there was still no guarantee I was going to find her. She could very well be at the house of a girlfriend or perhaps she had gone to watch a movie just to get away. There was really no way for me to know and I was wasting time and gas by driving up and down the main strip.

"There has to be another way..." I banged the steering wheel with my palm as if that would help me come up with a solution. Accidentally, I called up my contact book on the center console. Poppy's name was listed at the top as a favorite. Underneath it was, Ryan, my number two at *D &* *D*. It was then that an idea struck me.

I selected his number and crossed my fingers, hoping he would answer. After the third ring I was starting to lose hope, but then I heard his familiar voice. It was drowned out a bit by background noise, but just having him on the line was enough. "Ryan," I said. "I need you to do me a favor."

"What? I can't hear you."

"Where are you?"

"Digsters," he said. "You know, that bar down on Second Street with all the pool tables. I've been shooting some pool with your personal assistant, actually."

"Poppy's with you?" I make a three-point turn in the middle of a busy street, desperate to turn around and make towards *Digsters.* "Tell me she's still there with you, Ryan."

"She just left, actually. She said something about selling a ring. I thought it a little odd myself, but hey, who was I to get in her way? If you ask me, she seemed a little upset. Everything alright between you two?"

"Everything is fine – just something of a misunderstanding. I'll have it sorted out just as soon as I get her to answer her phone..."

The background noise died away, replaced with the occasional rush of a passing car. "She isn't answering your calls? But she was using her phone the whole time she was with me. Are you sure things are alright between you two? If there's anything I can do, just let me know." Ryan was an excellent person to have on a corporate team. He knew how to make hires and he was always brimming with innovation, but the guy couldn't play poker. His intentions were always written all over his face and I had seen the way he looked at Poppy. He wanted her. Well, he couldn't have her. This whole thing started off as an act, but it had become much more than that. In a few short weeks, she'd become a part of my life – someone to truly care about. I couldn't possibly let her slip through my fingers just because Neil had made me

look like the bad guy. I wouldn't let him ruin the best relationship I've ever had.

"Did she say where she was going?" I asked, but I didn't
need him to answer. It suddenly dawned on me where
Poppy would have gone.

Ends and Oddities.

19

POPPY

The sign on the door read 'closed,' but with all the lights still on, I decided to knock, hoping Odette would make an exception to her hours of operation for my sake.

I waited for what felt like an eternity. Raising on my tiptoes, I tried to see over the various shelves and displays, but there wasn't a lick of movement. My shoulders sagged with the heaviness of disappointment. I would just have to charge a hotel room to my credit card because I wasn't about to go back to the mansion and face Connor – not yet, anyway. My stomach was still twisted into a tight knot that threatened to make me sick.

Maybe I was the only one who felt the strong chemistry between us...

I knocked again.

Out of nowhere, Odette appeared. She was wearing an outfit of bright orange. It was burning my retinas just trying to look directly at her. All the same, I was glad to see her.

"It is late," she commented. "You should not be here. It was not written in the stars."

"May I come in?" I asked. "I have something I would like to sell."

"May I advise that you never sell something of value when you haven't had the time to think of life without its presence. Whatever is bothering you, my dear, it will come to pass."

"Please," I begged. "Just humor me. I don't really have anyone to turn to."

"I will not leave you out to the wolves." With that, she ushered me inside. I expected her to walk toward the counter, but she veered off track and took a seat on a rocking chair. She motioned to the matching pair. "Take a seat. It is easier to discuss issues of the heart while in motion." She proceeded to rock her chair, resting comfortably, eyes closed.

Thinking it futile to argue with the strange woman, I sat down. I was about to grab the ring when she placed her hand over mine. "You are here because of a misunderstanding."

"A misunderstanding?" I shook my head and pulled away from her touch. "No. I know what I saw."

"The mind has a way of coming to conclusions. Do not believe everything your head tries to tell you if your heart is saying something different. Often, it is the heart that is the wiser of the two."

"Listen to my heart?" It sounded like the kind of cheesy advice I might find rolled up in a fortune cookie. And yet, I could feel the tug of my heartstrings. From the start they had thought it impossible – that Connor would never turn on his word – would never go for a woman so base in character. "But how do I explain what I saw?"

"What did you see?" asked Odette. "What has brought you here?"

I held the ring in the palm of my hand. "I planned on selling this ring," I said. "Because this afternoon I saw Connor with another woman – the personal trainer who was here trying to argue that her bracelet was made with real diamonds."

The shop owner nodded her head. "Go on."

"She was straddled across his lap, tongue down his throat. I'm sure of it. I know what I saw." I clutched my hand into a fist. It was hard to look at something so beautiful when it meant nothing. "I know you don't know the story of our engagement, but let me just say that it is complicated, and I think I am done with it. I do not know what I was thinking when I agreed to be his wife, but I no longer feel right going through with the marriage. He isn't what I wanted."

Odette offered a sympathetic smile. "I think he is everything you wanted."

"No!" I got up, hands shaking by my sides. "He can't be when he's with someone else..." The tears threatened to overwhelm me, but I held them back. "On that night, I was looking for adventure – a change of pace. My best friend was getting married, about to start a new life with the love of her life and I was stuck in a rut, always the bridesmaid, never the bride. Honestly, I was sick of it. I think that's what made me go along with his crazy idea, but I never thought I would..." I couldn't say the word 'love' because it would hurt too much to admit it. "It was a mistake. All of it. I should have walked away while I had the chance, but now I'm in too deep. I can't stay here."

I tried giving Odette the ring. She refused to take it from me.

"That piece of jewelry is priceless. I cannot make an offer on it because it marks someone's love for you."

"Ha! You think Connor loves me?"

"It isn't a matter of opinion."

"What's that supposed to mean?"

"It means that I *know* he loves you."

"And how would you know that? Have you had a peek inside his head with a crystal ball? Or maybe you consulted the cards and they told you we were soulmates – destined to be. Well, it's all a bunch of bullshit and I'm not blaming you, Odette, because if there's anyone to blame here, it's me. I should have seen this coming from the start."

I was about to take my ring and leave when I heard the bell dinging from the front door.

Odette and I both turned around to see Connor walking through the door. "It isn't what you think." He reached us in a few short strides. "Just give me the time to explain."

I crossed my arms over my chest. "That's what you want, isn't it? You want me to let you weave your little story and come running back into your arms, but it isn't going to work. I know what I saw and there's no point in you wasting your breath trying to deny it."

"It was Neil."

That was certainly a response I wasn't expecting. "What are you talking about?"

"You saw my brother Neil. He's not very good at listening. I told him to stay out of my office and of course, that's the first place he goes."

"Why was Rhianna with him?"

"They are dating now," he said. "It was probably her idea to tag along. She probably thought it would make me jealous to see them together, but frankly, it just made me a little sad. My brother has always had ridiculously low standards, but this is a new record. I don't think he knows what he's gotten himself into. They won't last more than a week."

Connor was breathless like he'd been running a marathon. Slowly, he inched toward me, but he didn't dare make any sudden movements like he was afraid I might run away and never be seen again.

"Your twin, Neil..." I said aloud.

"Yes. As I swore to you before, I never have any intention of dating a woman like that. She isn't worth my time. But you – you're a different story." His hand found the side of my face, framing it with his palm. It was warm and just a little bit sweaty like he was nervous. "The day I met you, you caught my attention the second I looked your way. While every other girl ran around fretting about this or that, you had stolen the bride's bouquet, just trying to have a bit of fun. There wasn't a single moment when I saw you fuss over your hair or your makeup. You were confident and comfortable in your own skin and I loved that about you. I knew you were the kind of girl who would walk with her head held high."

He moved closer still. The heat coming from his body felt feverish like the words were burning him up from the inside.

"I can't explain the way you make me feel when you walk into a room, but it's like nothing I've ever felt before. It brightens my day. And when I have you in my arms? I can ask for nothing more. I'd give up everything I've ever worked for if it meant I could spend the rest of my life with you, hearing about your day and seeing the crinkle of your nose whenever you're focusing on something. Please," he breathed, "don't leave." His eyes bore into mine for a moment before he went for the kiss that changed everything.

He didn't need to say anything else because at that moment, my heart understood. Connor loved me just as much as I loved him. Maybe our time together was short and maybe the start of our relationship was a bit unorthodox, but that didn't matter because the chemistry was there and it would only grow stronger and bloom brighter with each passing day – each passing year.

We clung to each other like it was the only thing keeping us alive. Too caught up in the moment, I didn't hear the bell above the door. I don't think anyone did because the robber took us by surprise.

"Hands up! Don't Move!" he hissed from behind a mask. There was a gun in his hand, and he had it pointed at Connor. "Get away from the girl and stand over there." He pointed to the intended area, cocking the gun to make his demand all the more serious, but Connor did not move.

"You can have all the money in the cash box. There isn't much, but what's there is yours," said Odette, trying to address the issue at hand.

"Move!" the robber yelled at Connor.

"Okay, I'm moving, see? No need to point that gun at me. You're the one in charge here." Connor spoke calmly like he was one of those special forces cops trained to talk during hostage situations.

"That's right. I'm in charge here. Now, where's the money?"

"The cashbox is behind the counter."

"You." He pointed the gun at me. "Empty the cash register for me."

Connor glanced in my direction and gave the slightest of nods. This criminal was clearly deranged and for the sake of everyone's safety, it was best just to play along.

"Okay," I said, slowly inching towards the counter. He was right behind me, which made me nervous, but I reminded myself to stay calm. "Where do you want me to put the money?"

He grabbed a nearby shoe box, dumped the shoes, and handed over the box. "Here," he grunted. "Now, get a move on."

My hands trembled as I gathered the money. Poor Odette. The shop was her livelihood and this scumbag found himself entitled to take it all. What had he done to earn it? Absolutely nothing.

It became harder and harder for me to hold my tongue.

"Underneath, too," he said. "There's where all the big bills are kept."

I did what I was told, but as a stack of one-hundred-dollar bills went into the box, I lost my cool. "Robbing someone of their hard earned money won't solve your problems." The words were out of my mouth before I could stop myself from saying them.

The robber's eyes darkened as he cocked the gun. "What did you say to me, you little bitch?"

"You heard me. You're robbing this woman of money she worked hard for and you think because you have a gun you can just come in here and take that away from her?" Suddenly, I held the box behind my back. Something had possessed me in that moment. I wouldn't turn over the money. It went against every moral.

"I'll show you what this gun can do." Suddenly, he had his finger on the trigger and I was looking down a barrel. My life flashed before my eyes – the childhood fishing trips with my father – the pain in the ass braces I had to deal with during high school – but more than that, it was all the little conversations I had shared with Connor where, in the end, a simple smile said it all. Was I about to lose all that for my outspoken ways?

It happened in an instant. One second, everyone was still, the air tense. In the next, there was an explosion of movement. Connor went for the robber, tackling him to the ground. All I could do was scream. Out of the corner of my eye, I saw Odette run. A heartbeat later, the alarm went off. It was deafening, paired with a disco of red and blue lights. But above all the racket I heard the sound that turned my blood to ice.

Bang!

A stain of crimson seeped into the carpet. Who had gotten shot? I could barely see straight, but with Connor still struggling with the criminal, I knew I had to do something. How would I ever forgive myself if I stood by and did nothing while the love of my life died trying to protect me?

I grabbed whatever was closest to me – a vase. It could have been an heirloom worth a million dollars. At that moment I didn't care. My hands were sweaty as I adjusted my grip, readying myself to swing. I put my weight behind the blow praying I wouldn't hit Connor by mistake. The vase shattered on impact. There was a groan. The masked robber dropped into an unconscious heap.

With adrenaline still pumping through my veins, I grabbed something else, prepared to swing again should the thug so much as twitch a pinky, but he did not move. In the distance, I could hear the sirens. The police would soon arrive and take away the man that had threatened all our lives.

"Damn." Connor was sitting with his back against a nearby wall. He had his hand against his shoulder, which was painted a deep red.

"You're bleeding!" I was beside him in an instant, trying to survey the damage. I didn't know anything about gunshot wounds, but it looked pretty bad. "Oh, why did you have to go and play the hero?" Shaking as I was, I still managed to tear off a part of my dress and use it to apply pressure. He groaned, the pain intensifying at my touch. "I know. I know. You just have to stay strong for a little while longer until the ambulance gets here. They'll take good care of you. I prom- ise." My voice wavered as the tears started rolling down my cheeks. I could see just how pale he was becoming. His eyelids became heavy, head drooping forward. I was losing him. "No. Stay with me."

He blinked with eyes unfocused like he didn't quite know who he was.

"Connor!"

He did not respond.

My heart fell to the floor. Was he already gone?

20

CONNOR

I felt...strange.

There was pain radiating from my shoulder, but it had been numbed to some degree, leaving this tingling sensation just underneath my skin. I tried to move but nothing would budge. It was like there was this great weight bearing down on my arm keeping it stiff.

But there was something I could feel that was unmistakable – the warmth of Poppy's skin. She was holding my hand. I couldn't be sure, but I think she was talking, too. Was there someone else with her?

I opened my eyes and found myself in a hospital room. The ceiling looked like it was a thousand feet above my head. Everything else was a blur. No doubt they had pumped me with pain medication. Apparently, they weren't strong enough because when I went to turn my head, it threatened to burst with a jackhammer headache. Knowing I didn't want to experience that skull-splitting pain again, I kept still, letting my eyes close. The bright light wasn't doing me any favors either.

"He refused to move. It was idiotic but he placed his life before mine." Poppy's came through, clear as crystal. She was definitely recounting the events of the nights but to whom? The police? The doctors? "I never thought he would do something so reckless for my sake." Poppy squeezed my hand.

I wanted to return the gesture, but I was still too weak to move. How much blood had I lost? It felt like there wasn't a single drop left in my body.

Someone got up. I could feel them approach the bed. Their presence was accompanied by a familiar scent – maple syrup and pine.

Gramps? I wanted to speak, but with my mouth so dry, I couldn't part my lips to utter a single syllable.

"Connor was always a very ambitious lad. After his mother died and his father left to find another wife, he turned to hard work for distraction. He wanted to pull himself up by the bootstraps and make a place for himself in the world. Deep down, he was heartbroken that his father would abandon him, but I never did see him shed a tear."

"Neil was a different matter." It was my grandmother. Her voice was a bit raspy like she in the process of fighting off a cold. Lately, her health had taken a nosedive.

I felt guilty about postponing my trip to Maine. There was always so much work to be done and there was never a good time to go. Well, I didn't care what was on my schedule, I would *make* time.

"He was a sensitive boy. When his father left, he sobbed for days, begging us for answers, but of course, we couldn't tell him the truth. He became bitter – resentful – he stopped listening to us. It was quite a handful trying to raise that boy and yet, I fear, it wasn't enough. I've watched the two brothers grow apart and it kills me. I want nothing more than for them to laugh together like they once did – to put their differences aside and act like family."

There was a knock from somewhere in the room.

"Neil?" my grandparents said in unison.

"How is he?" Neil asked. "I heard about what happened. He's going to make it, right?"

"The doctors say he'll be fine. He might need a bit of physical therapy to get his arm back to full mobility, but the bullet failed to go through anything important, so he was lucky in that regard." As Poppy spoke, she brought a wet sponge to my forehead. It felt good against my burning skin.

I opened my eyes.

Poppy gasped. "You're awake." She blinked like she couldn't quite believe what she was seeing. "He's awake!"

I tried to smile but wasn't sure if I had managed it. Save for the throbbing in my temples, the rest of my face was numb.

Suddenly, Poppy had her arms around me.

I winced. The pain was enough to knock the wind right out of me, but I didn't want her to let go. It felt so good to know that she was safe – that I still had plenty of time to hold her and tell her how much I loved her.

"You had us worried for a minute there, sonny," said Gramps.

"Oh, Connor..." My grandmother started to cry, dabbing the corners of her eyes with my grandfather's hand-kerchief. "I don't know what I would have done..."

"Come on, Henrietta, let's give them some space." Gramps took her by the shoulders and away from the bed. I could still hear my grandmother crying while she was out of sight.

"How do you feel?" asked Poppy. "Do you want me to call the nurse?"

"In a minute," I said. "I need some time with my brother."

Poppy looked hesitant to leave me, but after a moment, she nodded her head and left my bedside, joining my grandparents.

"I want to know why you're here."

Neil rubbed the back of his neck and stood awkwardly at the foot of my bed. "You're my brother," was all he said in response. He had yet to look me in the eye.

I waited. For once, I wanted us to have a civil conversation. We had been at each other's throats for too long. It was time for us to make amends, for if getting shot had taught me anything it was a lesson of perspective. Time is too precious. Holding a grudge does nothing but waste the time you might spend with someone you love. "For what it's worth, I'm sorry," I said, breaking the ice. "I haven't always been the best brother and I realize that, but I've been a hardass all these years because I wanted you to be better – to set out and make something for yourself, but I never stopped to consider that maybe we're different people and just want different things in life."

Neil shook his head. "You shouldn't be the one apologizing. I've been a pain in the butt, I know that. I haven't been the greatest brother in the world, either, but I always felt like I was living in your shadow and it sucks to always feel like you're second best."

His words touched home. "I had no idea..."

"I'm not blaming you. I should have said something, but instead, I kept it all inside. I think that's why we drifted so far apart. But I'd like to put that all that behind us and start over. What do you say? Can we go back to being twins?" Neil held out his hand.

"Not going to happen," I said.

"What?"

"I'm not going to shake your hand. You're my brother, now come over here and give me a hug."

Neil chuckled. "Are you sure about that? I don't want to be responsible for your medical bills if I fuck you up."

"Shut up and come here." It felt good to make amends with my brother. Losing a twin to all the arguments had been like losing a part of myself. "Oh, and one more thing. I'm going to need you to be the best man at my wedding."

"You've got yourself a deal."

"Speaking of deals, I have an announcement to make." My grandfather had a voice that commanded attention. Everyone looked his way, waiting for whatever he was about to say next. "I've been made aware that your engagement with this young lady has been a ploy to get the family business from your brother because you thought that you'd be a better fit when it comes to managing the company. No offense to you, Neil, but I believe Connor is right. He has experience whereas you do not."

I saw Neil's shoulders sag.

"However, I run a family business and I intend to keep it that way. You two will own the company fifty-fifty and work *together*. Should there be any disagreement between the two of you, it is your problem to solve."

Neil and I exchanged a look. "What do you think?" he asked. "Would you mind having me as a business partner?"

"I might be tempted to throw you out a window a few times, but I think we can make this work." Everyone in the room laughed. "Oh, and we're going to have to buy you a suit. I can't have you running around in those skinny jeans. It would be a disgrace to the family name."

"Not going to happen," said Neil. "I'm not going to have you cramping my style. Besides, who says skinny jeans can't be a part of corporate casual?"

21

POPPY

"Mind if I give you a hand?" Connor's in-house nurse had just arrived to change his bandaging, and not wanting to get in the way I had snuck into the kitchen to find his grandmother peeling potatoes.

"Not at all," she said with a smile. "I'm making a pot roast. It used to be their favorite growing up. Hopefully, their tastes haven't changed over the years. It's really been quite a while since I cooked for the entire family. I miss when they were still just little tykes running around my skirt. Oh, we used to bake all sorts of things back then – cookies, cakes, cinnamon rolls."

I was happy to listen to Henrietta as she went down memory lane. It made me feel like I was getting to know Connor on a whole new level. Sure, I had seen him as a businessman and as a lover but never as a carefree child. "Were they troublemakers?" I asked.

"Most definitely," she answered. "When they put their heads together, they caused all sorts of havoc. They were inseparable during all their scheming." She seasoned the meat with a blend of different herbs and spices before putting it in the oven. "I truly hope that this is the start of their renewed friendship. It was always so heartbreaking to know that they were at odds with one another; I think family should always stick together." She cleaned her hands with a dishcloth before pouring a glass of wine for herself, reaching to grab another glass. "Would you care for some?"

"No, thank you." I finished peeling the potatoes. "How do you want these?"

"Just as they are is fine. I'm going to roast them with a butter garlic sauce."

"Sounds delicious." Passing on the wine, I grabbed a diet soda from the fridge.

"What about you, dear? Do you have any siblings?"

"None," I said. "Like Connor and Neil, my father left. My mother raised me as best she could, but she was a sick woman and never engaged in another relationship. She would always say that I was her number one priority, but I think she was just too exhausted to deal with the headache that comes with dating. By the time I was ten, her illness took a turn for the worse and I was often the one taking care of her. The only time I got to be a kid was when I visited my friend Jenna."

Henrietta nodded. "Sweet girl. I've only met her a half dozen times as her father tends to keep his distance. I think he regrets leaving the boys."

"It's strange how things work out, isn't it? What are the odds that I would fall for my friend's half-brother? I didn't even know Connor existed until the wedding."

"Some things are just meant to be," said Henrietta.

"So, you aren't upset that Connor and I faked an engagement to try and take the family business? I will be the first to admit that it was selfish on both counts. Connor thought himself better than his brother and I was hoping to snag myself a mansion. We were really making a disgrace of what marriage stands for."

"And now?"

I went to speak but couldn't, not quite sure what she was asking.

"Are you still hoping to snag yourself a mansion?"

"No," I answered without hesitation. "I couldn't care less about the mansion. All that matters to me is that I keep living alongside Connor. We could move to a cave with nothing but a fire between us and I'd still be the luckiest girl in the world. I never thought I would fall in love with him when we first made our little arrangement, but now there's no denying it. He's taken up residence in my heart and I never want him to leave that home. The only thing that scares me is that it all happened so quickly."

Connor's grandmother swirled her wine and took a sip. There was a shimmer to her eyes causing the flecks of gold around her irises to shine brighter. "I can tell you one thing – my grandson loves you. He risked his own life to keep you safe." She adjusted the temperature on the oven. "I've always been worried that his work would get in the way of him finding a partner. He drowns himself behind the desk, but I think he's finally found something more important than that."

I blushed. "Do you truly mean that?"

"I do." She placed her hand on my shoulder. "Welcome to the family, Poppy."

At that moment, I felt like I truly belonged. It was no longer a matter of pretending. Everything had managed to work itself out. The family business was being shared by the two brothers. Connor's grandparents were supportive of our relationship. And there was no longer any doubt in my heart regarding Connor's fidelity.

"I have a question."

"I might have an answer," said Henrietta.

"How did you know you were in love with your husband? That he was the man you wanted to spend the rest of your life with?"

"I just knew." She peered into the living room where the boys were playing cards. Connor seemed to be losing because there was a deep scowl on his face. Neil, on the other hand, had a pile of chips stacks on his side of the table. "It was like something had clicked. I can't really describe it, but I think you know what I mean."

"I do," I whispered. "It's like I've spent my entire life with this missing part of my soul and now, finally, it's whole. I'm exactly who I was always meant to be."

22

CONNOR

"Someone here is cheating," I said.

"Or perhaps your luck has run out. I mean, count your blessings. The bullet missed all the important parts of your shoulder. You really can't expect your luck to hold out for a poker game. It must be exhausted." Neil kept checking his cards even as he spoke. Either he had a really good hand, or he was trying to make us think he did. "But complaining isn't going to help you. Are you in or are you out?"

The odds were against me and I didn't want to risk playing a bluff, so I folded.

"How are you doing?" Poppy appeared with an ice-cold drink in her hand. "Sorry, it's just soda. With all the medication you're taking, I can't have you drinking alcohol."

"Do you really think a splash of rum is going to kill me?"

"I'm not about to take that chance," she said. "Now, are you boys almost done? The food is on the table. I might be wrong, but I don't think Henrietta is the kind of woman you want to keep waiting. I've seen the way she handles a knife."

I expected my grandfather to say something, but with

his face as blank as a piece of marble, he doubled his bet, waiting for Neil to counter. My brother grinned and pushed his whole stack of chips to the center of the table. "I'm all in."

"That's a bold move," said Poppy. "Are you sure you want to do that?" She had peeked over my grandfather's shoulder, seeing his cards.

"It's too late now." I leaned back in my chair waiting for the reveal. "Pocket aces," I said, slapping my knee as Gramps lay down his hand, a slightly bemused look on his face. "The old man still has the magic touch."

Neil looked thunderstruck.

"We are going to have to work on your poker skills before we get your working on any negotiations. If you jump into situations so eagerly, you're going to get burnt."

"Lecture me later." Neil was too bummed to listen to me. He dragged his feet into the kitchen. My grandfather was next to follow, leaving me alone with Poppy. It was the first time since the accident. As if we were both waiting for this moment, we leaned into one another, lips coming together in a sweetness that spoke of our future together – a future founded not on some scheme but on actual emotion.

"I'm sorry," I whispered. "It was stupid of me to fake an engagement."

She shook her head. "It was that stupid idea that got us under the same roof. Without it, who's to say we would be together now?" She kissed me again, our lips dancing to the tunes of our hearts. "I do not regret a thing," she said as she breathlessly pulled away, fingertips tracing the side of my face. "All I ask is that we change the terms of our agreement."

"Oh?"

"I don't want this mansion." She swept her arm around

us, motioning to all the luxuries that could have been hers. "All I want is to be wherever you are." She paused. "And maybe have you put in a good word with your grandmother so I can work at one of her salons."

"Do you not like working as my personal assistant?"

"I do, but life is too short for me to be doing anything other than what I love."

"I'm right here and yours for the taking," I said with a wink.

"You do realize that your family is in the other room, don't you?"

I wrapped my arm around her waist and pulled her close. "Sure, but there's one thing I have got to say before we join them."

"And what might that be?"

"I love you."

––––––––––––

"HOW NICE OF you to join us," said Neil. His plate was heaping with pot roast but he had yet to touch his meal. If I had to guess, my grandmother had threatened to hit him with a wooden spoon if he dared to start without me. "What were you two doing in there, anyway?" He was looking at Poppy who was red in the face. Hearing me say those three little words had nearly brought her to tears and I'll admit, hearing her say them back excited me in a way I wouldn't soon forget.

"Never mind that," my grandmother interjected. "Take a seat, both of you, before the food gets cold."

We did what we were told and for the first few minutes, no one said a word. Neil was stuffing his face. Poppy still had this dazed expression plastered on hers. As for my grandparents, I had never seen them look happier. No doubt, when they had taken the trip to California, they had thought it would end in tragedy – that they would find their grandson horribly injured, maybe even dead. Surely, they hadn't expected for my brother and me to make amends or for Poppy to be part of the picture. If I had known things would have worked out this way, I would have gotten shot long ago.

"I would like to propose a toast," I said, holding up my glass. "To family and whatever the future may bring to our table."

"Cheers." Everyone clinked their glasses around the table. I smiled at the sound because I knew it was the signal of a new start. I'd make my grandparents proud by carrying on the family business and I'd do so alongside my brother, learning to work with the differences that defined us instead of fighting against it and severing our bond. And Poppy? Well, I had a feeling that we were about to enter that honeymoon phase so many people like to talk about.

"ARE you sure you can't stay?" I asked. "There's plenty of room for you here."

My grandmother smiled knowingly. "That is very kind of you, Connor, but we've already booked a hotel room and if we cancel, we'll be responsible for paying some ridiculous fee and you know how your grandfather gets about fees."

I knew it was just an excuse, but I didn't argue with them.

"What about you, Neil? You're more than welcome to take one of the guest bedrooms."

"I think we'll be seeing a lot more of each other from

this point forward. I might be awesome, but there you know what they say—"

"Too much of a good thing," I said, finishing for him. It was like we were twins again. "Alright, then. I'll see you around. And do me a favor and dump Rhianna."

"Way ahead of you, man. I don't know what I was thinking with that one."

"I think it was just bad blood all the way around," I said. "But we're over that now, aren't we?"

"I'll think about it." We laughed as brothers should before hugging it out. It was like a weight had been lifted from my shoulders. I no longer had this darkness hanging about me. All was as it should be.

"Have a goodnight, everyone." I watched from the door until they had disappeared down the road. With their headlights no longer visible, I turned to find Poppy had disappeared. I thought I would find her in the living room, but all I found was the fireplace crackling with fresh wood. "Poppy?" I called.

I heard her footsteps.

Turning around, I was greeted by the sight of her wearing nothing but her silken robes. "What's this?" I asked.

"I thought I could help you relax a bit," she said, her voice a seductive whisper. "Sit down."

Who was I to argue with a woman so lovely?

She was careful while unbuttoning my shirt. "Let me know if I do anything to hurt your shoulder, but I promise to be extra gentle." With my torso exposed, she placed some lotion on her hands and ran them across my skin, kneading the flesh beneath her fingers until all the soreness of laying in a hospital bed for a few days melted away.

"You're too good to me," I murmured. "You really needn't do this."

"Connor, you saved my life. This is the least I can do." She brushed her lips against the side of my neck, lingering at my lobe. She nipped at it, pulling gently. "Although, I have to say that you were pretty dumb to play the hero like that. That guy could have killed you."

"And had I not done anything, he could have killed you, too. I just couldn't risk that happening," I answered. "I had known I loved you for a while, but just the thought of losing you pushed me over the edge. Of course, I wasn't thinking straight. Who does when there's a gun pointed at your dream girl?"

"You think I'm your dream girl?" She was working some kind of miracle on the small of my back.

"Yes," I moaned. "You're my dream girl."

23

POPPY

"Well, let your dream girl make your wildest fantasies come true." I had him turn over, so he was lying on his back. To make him more comfortable, I placed a pillow underneath his shoulder. "How's that?" I asked.

"Well, the view is great," he said with a laugh.

The sash around my robe had come undone and now it was hanging open, showcasing everything I had to offer. He feasted on my naked body. I could tell he was itching to touch – to grab at my backside – but he kept his hands to himself, letting me take the lead.

I shrugged off the robe and pumped a bit more lotion onto my palms. I made for his chest, but at the last second, I changed course, letting my hands explore the curves of my body. Connor watched with eyes wide and mouth hanging agape. I was giving him the show of the century and there was no way he'd miss a second of it. "Oh, if this is the kind of treatment I get after coming home from the hospital, I might consider saving your life more often."

"Don't even think about it," I said. "Seeing you covered in all that blood, it was the worst moment of my life. I never want to go through that again." I shimmied between his legs and pulled off his pants. "And who's to say this can't be a common occurrence. I think so long as you return the favor from time to time, I'd be more than happy to keep a bottle of lotion around the house."

"You strike a very tempting deal," he said. "I'm going to have to take you up on it."

"Good." I tucked my thumbs into the waistband of his boxers. Slowly, I pulled them off his hips. I could see the desperation on his face, but I didn't go any faster. "What's the matter?" I asked, pausing for his response. His cock, eager to come out and play, stood rock hard and pressing against the material of his boxers, pitching a formidable tent. I took his tip through the fabric and rolled it between my fabric.

He pushed his hips into the air in a silent plea.

Am I pushing him too far? I thought. *Maybe he deserves some slack after what he's been through...*

In the end, I decided it was too much fun toying with him. "Baby?" I cocked my head to the side, my voice innocent. "Do you want me to stop?"

"No," he said at once. "Don't stop."

At those words, I ripped off his boxers, letting them fly across the room. Now that he was naked, he was mine for the taking.

"Someone's excited to see me." I took his cock in my hand, squeezing it once before sliding up its length. My palms were still slick with lotion, making it easy to glide up and down. One hand proved not enough so I used both, pumping at a steady rhythm until I saw the ecstasy written across Connor's face.

I stopped suddenly. He opened his mouth to plead with me, but I was already ahead of him, my tongue darting forward to find his balls. I explored slowly, wanting to find every point of pleasure. They became like strings. I plucked them deliberately, making him sing for me and oh, what music it was.

"What are you doing to me?" He pulled at my hair, trying to get me to move somewhere else, but I wanted him to squirm – to beg me to stop. My tongue continued its journey around his balls, lapping at every inch. He groaned even louder.

I pushed his legs apart.

"What are you doing now?" he asked, craning his neck to see. I just grinned and moved my ass side to side, giving him something nice to look at. He dropped his head onto the couch and that's when I went for it. My lips were tight around his girth as I bobbed my head up and down. I concentrated my efforts on his tip first because I knew it would drive him crazy. "Poppy... fuck..."

I loved the sound of my name on his lips. I wanted to hear it again only louder.

So, I left the tip behind and sucked harder – deeper. His cock pushed to the back of my throat, making me gag. I pulled back slightly, exchanging depth for speed, and whatever I couldn't reach with my mouth I teased with my hands.

"Fuck," he said again.

I had stopped to run my tongue along his underside, taking advantage of how sensitive he would be. He shivered at my ministrations and even though he didn't say a word, I knew he wanted more. It was in the air – written in the lust that surrounded us.

Quickly, I returned to his balls only to come back up to his tip. He shook with the pleasure of it. "Feels good, doesn't it?" Before he could answer me, I was back at it, sucking him hard and fast. He twitched inside my mouth, a sign that he was getting close. Knowing I didn't want him to blow before I could enjoy myself, I changed positions.

I was no longer between his legs but straddling his lap. I had my wetness against him, allowing a taste of what was to come but not yet reaching the main attraction. He would have to wait a little longer.

Bearing my own weight with my right arm, I leaned down and kissed him. He grabbed my hair and intensified the kiss. It felt like fireworks between us and we were both ready for the finale.

I moved my hips so he could slip inside. We had kept apart for over a week. The doctor had made it clear that Connor was to refrain from laborious actively for the first couple of days after coming home. Well, I had waited forty-eight hours and I couldn't wait another minute.

Wet as I was, he slipped inside without an ounce of resistance. My body welcomed him, wrapping tight around him like it had no intention of ever letting go. "Will I hurt you if I put my hands here?" I asked, resting them on his chest.

"Not at all." His good hand was on my hip, trying to get me into rhythm. I complied with his request and began to lift myself off his length only to push back down a second later. I had to remind myself to take it slow because all I wanted was to go to town. "Fuck, Poppy, that feels so good."

I couldn't agree more. Connor filled my every inch. The pleasure was making me weak in the knees. I could barely keep myself going. He always made it look so easy, but things were different now that I was on top.

"Fuck," I moaned along with him, trying to keep my climax at bay. It was going to be a good one – I could feel it mounting like a wave about to crash into the surface.

Digging my nails into his chest, I forgot my promise to keep things gentle and slow. I just lost control, riding him for all that I was worth. The heat between us rose to a boiling point. I felt myself burning up as I continued a relentless rhythm. We were both getting close, too close.

At the very last second, I got off, rolling off the couch and onto the carpet, panting hard as the orgasm rippled through my body, leaving a contented smile on my face and a tingle to every inch of my skin.

Beside me, Connor groaned. He had made quite a mess upon his own stomach. I couldn't help but laugh. "Sorry about that," I said.

"Now I know how you feel."

"Stay there. Let me get a couple of tissues." When I returned, Connor was just as I had left him.

"That was amazing," he said, wiping himself clean. "What got into you? I wasn't expecting such a wild night."

"What can I say? I missed you." I took a seat on the couch and curled up with one of the fur blankets. The fireplace was burning low, casting shadows around the room. "Can you really blame a girl for finding you irresistible?" I rested my head on his uninjured shoulder.

He played with my hair and tried to use the remote with his other hand, but even the act of pushing a button seemed enough to send pain shooting through his arm. As soon as I felt him wince, I sat bolt upright. "You shouldn't push yourself," I chided. "You know you're still a long way from healing completely."

"I really don't think using the remote counts as pushing myself," he said.

I shot him a look.

"Fine, fine. I won't do it again, but I have a feeling that

this one-armed business is going to get pretty old. Why couldn't that robber have shot my left shoulder?"

"I don't want to hear you joking about that." I handed him a couple of pills and some water. "Here. You're overdue for these. I should have realized."

"Please, I'm a guy. Sex is the best medicine we could ask for."

"It's definitely the sweetest," I agreed. "But seriously, I shudder to think about how lucky you are to be alive. He could have shot you through the heart and then I'd be without a husband and father to my future children."

"What?"

I stammered, unable to answer him. I had blurted out that last bit without thinking.

"You want me to father your future children?" he asked after a horrible stretch of silence. "Did I hear you right?"

"Yes," I admitted. "I do. And I know it's too soon in our relationship to start thinking about kids–"

"No," he said, interrupting me. "It isn't because I've thought about it, too."

I stared, completely thunderstruck by his response. "You have? Seriously?"

"Seriously. It's time for me to settle down and there isn't anyone else I rather settle down with. I've spent plenty of time on my own. I'm sick of it. I just hope you never get sick of me."

"Never," I whispered. "For as long as I live."

He grabbed the end of the fur blanket and tugged on it. "Care to cuddle?"

"I can't exactly lay my head on your chest like I normally would."

"Of course you can. These pills work wonders. Trust me." He lifted his arm as high as he could get it, beckoning me into his embrace. "Come on, don't leave me hanging here."

I relented, being very gentle as I rested my head. The fireplace crackled. We watched it in a mesmerized sort of silence before I came to ask the question that was burning in my thoughts. "You said that you've thought about having kids with me. Tell me about it."

"Well, it happened over dinner one day. I just looked over at you and saw the way you were cutting your steak into bite-sized pieces like a mother might do for her child. So, my imagination took that thought and ran with it. All of a sudden, there you were, tending to our little boy, his eyes bright just like yours. And you had another one on the way, too. I was hoping it was a girl. I've always wanted a pair – a boy to play baseball with and a girl to protect and cherish."

"If we had a little girl, do you think she'd be a girly girl or a tom boy?"

"What were you when you were a little girl?"

"I was in my own little world back then. I liked playing with dolls, but if the weather was nice, I was just as eager to go fishing with my dad."

Connor squeezed me against his chest. I had told him the story about my father's passing one night when I was unable to sleep. He had listened to every word and rocked me the entire time.

"What about you?" he asked as he took my hand, letting our fingers lock together. As he waited for my answer, his thumb grazed the back of my hand. "What do you see in our future kids?"

"I see an incredibly smart boy just like his father and a girl who's going to be the apple of her father's eye."

He kissed the top of my head. "Let's make it happen."

24

CONNOR

It was my last day of physical therapy and I was glad for it. The sessions had helped ease the pain and stiffness from my shoulder, but they were awfully dull. "Well, best of luck to you," said the doctor. "And try to stay out of trouble."

"No promises there," I answered. "Thanks for everything. If I ever need more physical therapy, I know who to call."

Behind the wheel of my car, I flexed my fingers. There was still an ache, but it was minimal – something I could live with – and frankly, I didn't think it would ever go away. I kind of liked it because it was a constant reminder of what I lived for and who I sought to protect.

On my way home, I stopped by a florist. "I'm looking for a bouquet of roses," I said.

"What's the occasion?" asked the girl behind the counter.

"A surprise."

"A romantic surprise?"

"You guessed it."

She nodded her head and led me to a section of the store decorated with hearts of every size, some red, some pink. "Might I suggest a box of chocolates as well?" I considered their selection and picked out a small heart-shaped box. "Good choice. Let me wrap those up for you."

I returned to the car, placing the flowers and chocolates in the backseat. Knowing I had one more stop to make, I left the car running, the air-conditioning blasting. I didn't want the chocolates to melt.

Down the street, I walked into *Ends and Oddities*.

"You've redecorated," I commented just as soon as I spotted Odette's flamingo-colored outfit. "I like it."

"Had to move some things around when the carpet was replaced. I think the energy is much better now, don't you think? The spirits can roam freely about the objects – come and go as they please."

"Whatever you say, Odette." I had learned it was better just to humor her. If I spoke a word of science she would hear nothing of it, so there was really no point in wasting my breath. Besides, I had come to like her quirky personality. "Anyway, I'm looking for a necklace."

"Is today finally the day?" she asked, clapping her hands together.

"I don't know what you're talking about."

"I've read your horoscope and it said that you are about to put things into motion. Today must be the first piece of the puzzle."

"Those two metaphors don't–" I shook my head, deciding to drop the argument I was about to make. "But yes, today I have set things in motion. I've decided on a wedding date."

"Does Poppy know?"

"It'll be a surprise. I plan to tell her when I give her the necklace."

Odette clapped her hands once more, obviously pleased. "Tell me more." She was opening and closing various display cases and stacking necklaces on the counter. I examined some of them, but I had a feeling that she hadn't yet found what she was looking for.

"Well, I haven't kinked out any of the details. I figure Poppy will want to have a hand in all that."

"Smart man." She paused, looking deep in thought. Suddenly, she dashed to some crevice of the store.

I continued my story knowing my voice would carry. "But I managed to get a date at the church where my grand-parents got married. I've always admired their dedication to one another and thought it would be the perfect tribute. Besides, I think Poppy will appreciate a Maine getaway – a nice cabin in the woods, maybe a bit of hiking, a few days out on the sea, fishing rods in hand."

"Sounds lovely. I'm sure she'll love it and I think she'll love this, too." Odette had returned with a simple black box. I took it from her and pulled off the cover. It was a pearl necklace.

"This is perfect," I said. "I knew I could count on you, Odette."

She smiled. "I look forward to the wedding."

"Look for your invitation in the mail."

"Oh, I will."

"WHAT'S THE OCCASION?" asked Poppy when I asked her to get dressed up. "Where are we going?"

"Remember the day I got shot?"

"How could I ever forget?" She was arranging the roses into a vase. "These roses are beautiful, by the way."

"They've got nothing on you, baby." I wrapped my arms around her waist and held her from behind. "And, as I was saying, if you remember the day I got shot, we were supposed to go down to the playhouse together. Well, that never happened. Time to change that." I pulled out the tickets and showed them to her. "I would suggest you get a move on because the show starts at seven and we wouldn't want to be late."

"Fine, but only if you join me in the shower."

"Given a deal like that, you don't leave me much choice." And so, I allowed her to drag me into the bathroom. Despite the countless times I had seen her naked body, there was still always a thrill that washed over me whenever I saw the perkiness of her breasts or the smoothness of her thighs. I swear she was becoming more beautiful with each passing day like a fine wine growing better with age. I could only imagine how I would feel after our fifth anniversary or even our fiftieth.

But what blew me away that night was not her body covered in droplets of water, cheeks rosy, hair wet and wild – it was when she dawned the vintage dress my grandmother had sent for her birthday. It suited her so well, I never wanted to see her wearing anything else. "I'm speechless," I said.

She spun in front of the mirror, letting the dress flare about her legs. "It feels like it was made for me."

"Maybe it was."

"And how would your grandmother have figured out my measurements?"

"You work at one of her salons now. Maybe she has someone spying on you."

"You're sounding like Odette." She slapped my chest.

I took the opportunity to grab her. "I would kiss you right now if it wasn't for that lipstick."

"It's kiss-proof," she said. "Or at least, that's what it claims to be. Should we test it out?" Before I could protest, she took my face in her hands and kissed me. If we didn't have a show to catch, I would have thrown her onto the bed right then and there. Oh, how she liked to tempt me with those sweet, sweet lips of hers.

Despite the pressing hour, the kiss continued.

I pressed her into the wall, my lips smashed into hers. I just couldn't get enough. It was like I was an addict desperate to get my fix.

It was only the burning in our lungs that prompted us to break away. "Hmm, it looks like it actually is kiss-proof. There isn't a speck of red anywhere on your face."

"And you still look perfect." I kissed her forehead, laced her fingers with mine, and pulled her from the bedroom.

In the car, I played her favorite album, a violinist who took the classic instrument and added a modern twist to it by adding electronic elements. I'll admit, I was a bit skeptical at first, but I was growing to like the genre.

"So, if I remember correctly, you've never been to a playhouse before. Why's that?"

"Well, nothing this fancy," she said. "I went to this really small playhouse this one time, but the show was complete garbage. I never went again. Besides, it was kind of awkward going on my own while none of my friends were interested in the performing arts. If they were going out on a Saturday night then they'd want to go to a party or something. Watching some play would have been considered a waste of time."

She placed her hand on mine and smiled.

"But I'm glad I now have someone I can go with."

"Of course." I brought the tips of her fingers to my lips and kissed them. "I was in a similar situation. My brother thought it stupid that I was such a fan of the fine arts when I should have been watching the game."

"You and your brother are worlds apart, aren't you?"

"You have no idea."

"Well, as far as I'm concerned, I have all the time in the world to learn about every little thing that makes you different from your brother. Every day, I hope to learn something new about you."

I smiled at the thought. "Even if we live to be 99?"

"Especially if we live to be 99."

"THAT WAS FANTASTIC." We were waiting for the valet service to bring back my car. "I'm really glad we came."

I took off my jacket and draped it over her shoulders. "I knew you would like it."

The car arrived. I immediately stepped forward and opened the door for her. "After you, my lady."

"You're up to something," she said. "You're acting like someone who has a secret."

"I don't know what you're talking about." I closed the door and tipped the valet driver before taking the keys. "Anyway, I hope you're hungry."

"We're going to dinner, too? Okay, you're definitely up to something."

"You act like it's a crime for me to treat my fiancée to a date night. If you want, we can go back home. As far as I'm concerned, I'm happy just as long as I'm with you."

She smiled. "If you're trying to make my heart melt, it's working. When did you get to be so sweet?"

"Maybe it was that box of chocolates," I said. "I ate most of the chocolate when you weren't looking."

"You didn't!"

I tried to keep the guilt from my face but one look in her direction had me laughing. "I didn't think you'd be so devastated. I'll tell you what. I'll buy you another box of chocolates on our way back from the restaurant."

"Score." She pumped her arm through the air, looking genuinely excited. It was little things like this that made me fall in love with her each and every day. "So, what restaurant are we going to? Do they have burgers?"

"You know, most girls would be asking for Italian or something outrageously expensive."

"Yeah, but you know I'm not like most girls. If I was, I don't think we'd be dating."

"You've got a point there." I took her hand and kissed the tips of her fingers. "I really can't tell you how happy you've made me, Poppy. Every day feels like a dream when I'm with you."

I should have seen it coming. "There," she said, grinning. "Proof that you aren't dreaming."

"You really didn't have to pinch me. It's just an expression."

"Wouldn't you rather be certain I was real?" she asked before toying with the radio. She wasn't able to settle on a station in the time it took me to drive to the restaurant. For the most part, Poppy was decisive and sure of herself, but that all went right out the window whenever music was involved. She didn't know what she liked, and I was lucky if we made it through an entire song. The DJ at our wedding was going to have a hell of a time trying to please her.

"We're here," I said.

"You know me so well."

It was a small mom and pop pizza shop just like the one we'd snuck off to during Jenna's wedding. "The internet tells me that this place makes the best thin crust in town."

"We will see about that." Poppy had no qualms about marching into a casual pizza parlor wearing an expensive dress. Sure, she got some funny looks from some of the other diners, but she didn't let it bother her. She just held her head high and proceeded to order a large pizza, claiming she wouldn't share a single bite with me.

"I didn't know you were so hungry," I teased.

"Famished," she said.

"So, we're really going to order two large pizzas between us?"

"Hey, I'm okay with leftover pizza for breakfast."

"I like the way you think."

Soon, we were laughing and having a grand ol' time. The night flew by as I became drunk on the happiness that came with spending time with my future wife.

"I think we should go. They look like they want to close up shop," observed Poppy. "Come on."

"Wait." I grabbed her by the wrist and got her to sit back down. "There's something I want to give you before we leave."

"Oh?" she cocked her head to the side.

I placed the necklace box on the table. "Odette helped me pick it out. If she were here, she'd probably say that you were destined to have it."

"What is it?"

"Open it." I pushed the box toward her and watched as she carefully pulled off the lid.

She gasped the second she saw it, bringing her hands to

her mouth. "Oh, Connor, it's gorgeous!" Seeing as she was stunned into a sort of paralysis, I took it upon myself to grab the string of pearls and clasp them around her neck. They rested perfectly on her collarbone. I had to agree with Odette – they were made for her. "I didn't think it was possible, but you look even more beautiful."

She touched them with the very tips of her fingers like she thought they might disappear if she applied any amount of pressure. "But why are you giving this to me?"

"What? I can't get my fiancé nice things?"

"I'm not complaining," she said. "But you usually have a reason for everything you do."

"You're right about that." I directed her attention to the box. "Maybe there's something you missed."

It was then that she noticed the slip of paper. "It's a date."

"The date of our wedding," I whispered against her ear. "Our future anniversary."

EPILOGUE
POPPY

That date came faster than I thought. It seemed to happen in the blink of an eye. One second I was having pizza with Connor and in the other, I was dressed all in white.

"Take it easy with those. You wouldn't want to show up to your wedding drunk, would you?" Jenna took the glass of champagne from my hand. "I don't know what you're so nervous about. You love him, don't you?"

"I do."

"See? Nothing to worry about." Jenna was much more pleasant as a bridesmaid. "Now, turn around so I can tighten your corset."

"Is that really necessary? I can barely breathe as it is."

"If I don't tighten your corset, then there's a good chance the dress will slip off as you're walking down the aisle. Now, I know you've always been proud of your girls, but I don't think it would be very appropriate to show them off to an entire church congregation, nor do I think your new husband would appreciate such a thing happening."

"When did you become so logical?" My voice sounded

snappy. "Sorry. I guess I'm just a little nervous. I don't mean to take it out on you."

Odette came into the room. She looked like a walking highlighter. "Ah," she said. "Getting those marriage jitters, are we? It happens to every woman."

"Even you?"

"Even me," she said with a laugh. "I was so terrified on my wedding day that I actually escaped through the bathroom window."

"You were a runaway bride?"

"Something like that." She waved her hand. "Can you call me a runaway bride if I failed to successfully run away? My husband found me in the park and the officiant married us right then and there. It was in the papers and everything."

"Don't get any ideas," said Jenna. "I'm not running to the park in these heels. Besides, with a train this long, I don't think you'd get very far before snagging on something."

"Right."

"How is everything in here, dear?" Henrietta peeked her head through the door. "Oh my." Her eyes glassed over with tears. "That dress looks better on you than it did on me."

"Thank you again for letting me wear it."

"The craftsmanship is exquisite," commented Odette. "They just don't make dresses like this anymore." She took my arm and examined the beadwork along the sleeve. "Really, this is a dress for the ages." Odette continued to mumble to herself, getting lost in some story or another.

"I should be the one thanking you," said Henrietta. "You've made my grandson very happy. More than that, I think you're the reason why Connor and his brother have rekindled their relationship. You should see them. They are joking around like a couple of teenage boys out there."

"Connor isn't nervous?" I asked.

"Oh, I'm sure he is, but he has always hidden it well." She handed me my bouquet. "But the time has come for you to go out there. Everyone is waiting for you."

"Right." I nodded my head in agreement, though my body didn't seem to get the message. It felt like my feet had been glued to the ground. More than a year ago, I had been bored and single, just looking for a bit of adventure. I took the risk of a lifetime agreeing to marry a stranger. But Connor was no longer a stranger. I had come to know everything that made him exactly who he was. I knew the exact pitch of his laugh and how he took his coffee in the morning. I could tell you his favorite type of cereal and his worst nightmare. He had opened up his heart to me and I had done the same, making myself vulnerable to his love because I knew he would never turn around and hurt me.

So, why was I nervous? "Alright," I said. "Let's do this."

I waited for the organist to start playing that iconic song. Only then did I step through a set of oak doors and into the church. It was beautifully decorated with streamers of white and blue. Family and friends lined the pews. Odette could be seen for miles. I focused on her friendly face for the first half of my walk and reminded myself to just place one foot in front of the other.

At one point I could no longer ignore his stare. It seemed to penetrate deep into my soul. I looked up, eyes locking with my husband-to-be.

I stopped in my tracks because I had never seen him look so handsome. The dark blue suit complemented his skin. He was cleanshaven and just the angle of his jaw was enough to make me weak in my knees.

"Keep going," urged Odette.

But I couldn't. It felt like I was being dealt too good a hand. How in the world had I gotten lucky enough to score a man who could make my heart soar with a single smile – who knew my every insecurity and exactly what kind of stupid joke would make me laugh? He was the guy I had been waiting for all my life – sweet, funny, and incredibly sensitive. His devilish good looks was the cherry on top because he had everything else.

I took a shuddering breath and waited. I feared everything would disappear before my eyes but there he remained, standing proud at the altar. He smiled and stepped down, meeting me at the aisle, hand outstretched in invitation. "Marry me," he said.

And I did.

I really couldn't tell you what the priest said, but there I stood, hand in hand with my fiancé. He kept a firm grip as if to say *I'm here.*

"Now to exchange vows."

That word – vows – was the signal I had been waiting for. My spine went as straight as a rod as I focused as best I could, knowing I would need to repeat whatever the priest said. As it turned out, it was easier than I thought. Connor messed up more than I did. Maybe he really was nervous under that cool façade.

Neil handed over the rings.

"I bless these rings as symbols of your everlasting love. With them, you will be bonded." The priest glanced at his book, but I was sure he had this part memorized. "And so, I ask you, Connor Dresden, do you take Pomona Merritt to be your lawfully wedded wife, to love and to hold until death do you part?"

"I do," he said.

"And do you, Pomona Merritt, take Connor Dresden to be your lawfully wedded husband, to love and hold until death do you part?"

"I do." Getting the ring on his finger was the hardest part of the whole ceremony.

"You may now kiss the bride!"

Connor swept me off my feet and planted the kiss of a lifetime. I really can't explain it other than the fact that it was fucking amazing. It did more than take my breath away – it had me reeling – head spinning – heart halfway to the moon.

The whole congregation cheered as Connor continued to turn my body to putty. If he hadn't be holding me, I would have fallen right on my ass.

His eyes were bright when he finally pulled back. "How does it feel to be Mrs. Dresden?"

"Like it was always meant to be this way," I said, a little breathless.

With our hands locked together, we ran down the aisle. Outside, everyone was waiting to rain down rice on our heads. Doves were released into the air as we made our way along the well-wishers, thanking them for their time.

By some miracle, we made it to the vintage car Connor had bought as something as a wedding gift. The plan was to teach me to drive and then the car would be mine. I had a feeling it would be a while before I felt comfortable getting behind the wheel of something so valuable, but until then, Charles, the chauffeur who had once saved me a lot of embarrassment, would be at my service.

Speaking of Charles, he had exchanged his usual uniform for a light blue suit. "Congratulations," he said. "I'm happy to see you two finally tying the knot. It's been a long time coming."

I smiled at my husband. Even though there was a ring on my finger, and we were on our way to take photos, it still felt so surreal.

"I haven't had the chance to tell you this, but you look absolutely stunning in that dress." He placed his hand at the back of my neck and kissed me. Somehow, his kisses felt different now that we were husband and wife. They were sweeter, and they were pretty damn sweet before.

"Did you see your grandmother crying?" I asked once we had settled back into our seats.

"She wasn't the only one. I was scared Odette was going to drown. Who knew she could be so emotional?"

I laughed. "I can't wait to see her out on the dance floor."

Connor laughed. "I just hope our videographer gets it on tape."

"I'm not leaving them a tip if they miss it."

Charles was taking the scenic route as per our request. Through the window, I was able to appreciate the beautiful Maine landscape. After a nightmare of logistics, we had managed to get *D & D* to move its headquarters to Augusta. It would be a phased move meant to make the whole thing as painless as possible, but I had my fears that there would be a few hiccups along the road. Thankfully, Connor no longer had to deal with such things on his own. After Neil proved to be worth his weight in gold, Connor took him on as partner for his own company. Apparently, all Neil needed was a bit of guidance and encouragement. He was even proving to be more of a workaholic than his brother.

"I can't wait until we live here," I said.

"Construction should be done on the cabin by the time we come back from our honeymoon."

"And if a bear tries to invade the house, will you protect me?"

"I took a bullet for you, baby. What's a bear?" I smiled and leaned my head against his shoulder knowing that I would always be safe in his arms.

"Hey, Connor?"

"Yeah?"

"I love you."

"I love you, too." He kissed the top of my head. "And I always will, but do me a favor and try to stay away from the bears. I would rather keep the integrity of my face. Taking a bullet in the shoulder is one thing but getting mauled by a bear is another."

I laughed. "I'll try, but I can't make any promises."

"I had a feeling you were going to say that," he said. "I guess if it comes down to it, your safety matters more to me than a good mugshot. Promise you'd still love me?"

"Now that's a promise I can keep."

— THE END —

XOXO, WINTER

Sometimes, you have to let fate carve out a path and see where it follows.

But taking that initial leap of faith is difficult when you've tumbled in the turmoil of your past and you know just how much it hurts to relive it.

I get it.

I've been there.

I've made my fair share of mistakes when it comes to the dating department.

And as far as I'm concerned, most men are complete assholes.

So why should I waste my mine?

It'll always end the same.

. . .

Or, at least, that's what I kept telling myself as I kept my head down and focused on becoming a veterinarian.

Forget them, I repeated over and over again.

You don't need them.

How many times have you cried for them and they never shed a single tear for you?

Maybe that voice in the back of my head had a point but what's the point of living if you're always on your own?

Because, trust me, being alone sucks.

And the constant silence of an empty apartment is a surefire way to insanity.

So, why am I so opposed to Dr. Goodman?

The dreamboat that fell out of the sky and practically landed on my lap due to a little airplane mix up.

Because I'm afraid that he's going to turn out like every other lowlife that's ever shown their interest in me.

And I'm not about to get my heart broken by a surgeon even if he knows how to stitch it back together again.

I think I'll just save myself the pain.

1

WINTER

"I'm going to miss you, honey!" My mother engulfed me in one of her world-famous bear hugs. I could no longer breathe. "Promise you'll come back to visit me really soon!" To my dismay, she hugged me even harder. "Oh, and good luck with school. I know you'll do great!"

I tried to say something but with my lungs flattening into pancakes, it was impossible.

"You'll be a vet in no time and then maybe you can get a job down here next to me. I know the local–"

"Mom!" I said at last. "I need to go or I'm really going to miss my flight."

"Oh!" She lunged forward and again I was left gasping for air.

Her new boyfriend came to my rescue. With a hand on her shoulder, he managed to pull her back. I nodded in his direction before making my getaway.

"Passport, please." The TSA agent looked like he was bored out of his mind.

I rummaged through my bag but like the black hole it

was, it had managed to consume my passport. "Great," I mumbled under my breath. "Just great."

"Is there a problem, ma'am?"

"No, no, just...give me a second." I could feel the heavy stares of everyone behind me.

"Most of us don't have all day," he said. "If you can't find what you're looking for, I'm going to have to ask you to step aside."

"*Now boarding flight A7. All passengers for A7 please check-in before boarding.*"

"Shit." I plopped my bag onto the counter and tore through it in a desperate attempt to find what I was looking for.

"Ma'am—"

"Here." I practically shoved my passport in his face. "And if we could hurry this up a bit... my flight is about to board."

"That's not my problem. Passengers are advised to arrive at the airport two hours before their flight time."

Well, you don't have a mother that takes a literal eternity to get ready in the morning.

"Hmm..." he mused.

"What is it?"

"Seems like your flight has been overbooked."

"Overbooked?" I repeated. "What do you mean it's been overbooked?"

A random flight announcement pinged over the intercom system, halting his ability to answer my question.

He was just about to say something when yet another announcement was made. "*Final call for passengers boarding flight J15 to Toronto, Canada—*"

I held my breath. Would there be another? Would I ever be able to walk away from this ticket counter?

The attendant waited for a beat but then, finally, answered me. "There are too many people on the plane."

"Wait... so what does that mean?" The hustle and bustle of the airport was starting to make my head spin.

"It means we'll have to put you on another flight."

"Another flight?" I gripped the counter. "When do you imagine that'll be?"

"Well, from the looks of it, the next flight back to Maine leaves in two hours or so. Or, you can wait five hours and ride first class."

"Did you say first class?"

"Mhm."

"You mean the front of the plane where you have all that leg space and the stewardesses serve complimentary champagne, right?"

"That would be correct."

"And...how much would that cost?"

"Nothing more than the original price of your ticket. The airline assumes responsibility for overbooking. Consider this our apology."

"Deal," I said a heartbeat later.

The TSA agent took down all my information and typed it like a sloth. You'd think that someone who worked with computers all day would be able to type just a little bit faster.

"Alright, you should be all set. You're on flight M22." He handed over a printed ticket. "Your gate will be announced over the loudspeaker but as of right now it is expected to be H9."

"H9," I repeated. "Got it." With that, I spun on my heels and off I went.

"Ma'am."

I froze.

"Your passport."

"Right." I doubled back, snatched it up, and shoved it into my purse. From there, I went straight through security. *With all the fancy technology these days, why do we still have to go through the hassle of taking off our shoes?* Like many other people, I struggled to carry my luggage to a nearby bench. I was a mess. Despite packing 'light,' it still felt like I had all of Manhattan tucked away inside my backpack.

Calm down, I told myself. *You've got five hours to kill. There's no need to rush.*

Agreeing with that little voice in my head, I decided to explore some of the duty-free shops. Some of them made little sense to me. Why would anyone need to buy designer luggage when they're already at the airport? And did anyone actually drop a few thousand bucks on top-of-the-line laptops while traveling from point A to point B? Maybe that's just something you do when you're rich.

"All passengers of flight T11, please be advised that your gate has now changed—"

I was so focused on listening to the announcement that I ended up bumping into someone. The backpack I wore threw me off balance and I felt myself falling back like a turtle about to land on its shell. I braced myself for it but instead of making an idiot of myself, someone grabbed me before my feet could slip from under me. His grip was strong as it tightened around my arm.

"Are you alright?" he asked.

I blinked and looked up at what must have been a model or something. *Oh my.*

"Miss, are you alright?" he asked again, this time leaning down so his face came dangerously close to mine. *Oh, c'mon, say something, Winter.*

"I'm f-fine," I stuttered. *Great, now this guy probably thinks I have some kind of problem.* "I'm fine," I repeated as if that would make things better. "Totally fine." *Okay, now you're totally drooling over this guy. Get a grip!*

But that was incredibly hard to do when this guy looked like he belonged on the big screen. Hey, for all I knew, he was probably a movie star or something. With a smile like that and hair that thick and luxurious... And don't even get me started on that body. Tall. Broad shoulders. A tapered waistline. This guy had it all.

"Good," he whispered, his voice as smooth as whiskey.

Was this guy trying to make me melt right now?

"Who knew buying some snacks could be so dangerous?" He chuckled.

Oh, jeez, he even has a gorgeous laugh.

"Right."

"I try and eat healthily but as soon as I see chocolate, that all goes out the window." He bent down and browsed the candy bar selection. His thighs were so sculpted they looked like they were going to burst through his dress pants as he squatted down.

For some crazy reason, I squatted down next to him. I had no right talking to this guy, but I wasn't about to waste this once-in-a-lifetime opportunity. "So, you have a bit of a sweet tooth then?"

"That's the understatement of the year," he said. "If it weren't for some incredible dentists, I doubt I would have any teeth left."

"That bad, huh?" My initial jitters were starting to fade, and I found it easier to talk to this guy.

"Oh yeah."

"So, what would you recommend? The king-sized Snickers or the king-sized Milky Way?"

"Oh, Milky Way all the way. That's not even a question worth asking. Snickers has always been a pet peeve of mine. It's just not enjoyable. Those nuts are like putting M&Ms in soft serve ice cream – hard and impossible to eat. I'd probably be better off eating a mouthful of rocks."

"Wow... I didn't know anyone could be this passionate about candy." It was only after I picked up the Milky Way bar that I realized I had spoken my thoughts aloud. *Great, way to insult the guy.*

He rubbed the back of his neck. "Some may call it a problem."

"I didn't mean it like that," I said, trying to rectify the situation but I felt like I was only making things worse.

"Don't worry about it." Our steps coincided as we approached the cashier. There was a long line trailing around the store. "You'd think they'd have more people working here. It's the most popular store in the whole airport."

"Yeah, because why spend your money on gourmet seafood when you can waste it on an overpriced bag of Doritos?"

"You mean Flemings? They actually have pretty good food there," he said without missing a single beat. "I don't know if its gourmet, per se, but it's not half bad."

My jaw nearly hung agape. This guy had actually eaten there? Flemings was one of those restaurants that omitted the prices on their menus so they could slap you with an outrageous bill at the end of your meal. Only those with a few hundred to blow ever stopped to eat there. Maybe this guy really was a movie star. As subtly as possible, I glanced at what he was carrying. A designer luggage bag. From the looks of it, the thing was made of genuine leather. On top of that bag sat a plastic one from the tech shop. Was that... no... it couldn't be...

A brand-new computer.

This guy was *definitely* loaded.

"So, what were you doing in Florida?" he asked.

"I came to visit my mom. She lives in Clearwater with her new boyfriend."

"Ah," he nodded. "You fond of him?"

I shrugged. "He's one of the better ones so I guess I can't complain. For the most part, they left me alone as I lounged by the pool."

"Doesn't sound too bad."

"Oh, no, it was a much-needed break from everything."

He raised an eyebrow in question. *I've always wanted to do that, and this guy makes it look so damn easy.*

"I'm studying to become a vet but it isn't easy. Just trying to afford all my textbooks has me working two jobs. Plus, I volunteer at the pet shelter whenever I have a bit of free time under my belt."

"Sounds like you're a busy woman," he said as we crept forward. It didn't look like the counter was getting any closer.

"You could say that."

"Well, I think you can do it." He rested a hand on my shoulder and squeezed it gently. Now, when a random stranger touches you like that, it's usually a little weird but with this guy, it felt...natural. A sort of tingle crept up my spine and settled inside my chest. "I know what it's like to stay up all night studying. Sometimes, all you want to do is give up but, in the end, it'll all be worth it."

"Sounds like you're speaking from experience."

"Doctor," he explained. "Well, surgeon, to be specific. I specialize in cardiology."

"Wow, that's impressive."

He smiled. "As long as I can help save people, I'm happy."

So, this guy is smoking hot and altruistic? Could he get any more perfect?

Finally, we reached the counter. I placed my bundle of snacks down and rummaged through my purse, searching for my wallet. Before I could find it, my new acquaintance slipped his card through the reader.

"Why did you do that?" I asked.

"Consider it my good deed for the day," he said with a wink. "Now you can put that towards a textbook."

"Thanks." Already, my cheeks were burning.

"Anyway, I had to chug down a giant bottle of water before going through security so you'll have to excuse me." And with that, he hurried off towards the bathroom. I never even managed to snag his name.

Good going, Winter. That was your one chance to snatch up a handsome doctor and you blew it.

My shoulders sagged, knowing that I would probably never see him again.

Oh well.

"Flight B6 has been delayed!"

Fearing that something had happened to my new flight, I checked the status of it and found that it was still expected to arrive on time. Pleased, I headed over to the proper gate and sat down next to one of the large windows. The Florida sunlight felt nice and warm against my skin. I would miss it as soon as I arrived back in Maine's frigid climate.

At least I get to fly back in style.

And with that thought, I ripped open my Milky Way and enjoyed the sweetness.

2

———

WINTER

A *few hours later.*
       I blinked into consciousness to find the gate was now filled with passengers. They were all sitting on the edge of their seats like they were ready to stampede into the plane.

What time was it?

I looked at my phone.

3:45.

My eyes widened. The plane was due to leave in five minutes.

"Now boarding flight J3," announced the woman at the counter.

Wait... J3? That didn't sound right at all.

Quickly, I dug up my ticket and tried to find the flight number. Why did they have to put so much useless information on such a tiny piece of paper? And why were the flights and gates all numbered the same way? Were they actively trying to confuse passengers?

Flight M22. So...if all these people are waiting for flight J3, where the hell is my plane?

I jumped to my feet and grabbed all my stuff. Thankfully, the zipper to my backpack was done up because it now hung upside down from the crook of my arm. "Excuse me!"

The woman behind the counter looked up and offered a professional smile. "Yes?"

"Do you know where I would find flight M22?"

"M22?" she repeated like I was speaking some foreign language.

"Last call for all those boarding flight M22. Again, this is the last call for all those boarding flight M22 out of gate K8."

"Where's gate K8?" I asked.

"On the other side of the airport," the woman frowned. "I don't know if you'll make it—"

I didn't wait for her to finish. I took off at a mad sprint down the hallway. Countless people gasped as I nearly bumped into them but at this point, I didn't care. Even if security started chasing me with their Segways, I wasn't about to stop. I wasn't about to miss my chance to ride first class.

By the time I reached the gate, they were about ready to close the aerobridge. "Wait!" I called out as I waved my ticket in the air. The stewardesses exchanged an annoyed look, and for a second I thought they'd turn me right around, but to my relief I was allowed inside the claustrophobic tunnel.

I really hate these things, I thought as every step felt like I was walking on a row of swings. *Couldn't they make this thing just a little more stable?*

Thankfully, I reached the plane sooner than expected. Another stewardess was there to greet me. As soon as she saw my first-class ticket, her whole demeanor changed. She treated me with the utmost politeness as she directed me to my seat.

Oh, it was truly a thing of luxury. I ran my hands over the suede and it felt so *soft*. You might think you know soft, but you've never felt anything quite like this. Trust me.

"Here, let me." The stewardess tucked my luggage into the overhead compartment. "You can keep your purse and backpack on hand if you'd like. There's more than enough room under the seat in front of you."

"Thank you," I said.

I plopped down and I practically melted into the seat. It was warm but the air was nice and cool, making it just right to cuddle up underneath a blanket. The stewardess seemed to read my mind because she already had one in hand. "If there is anything we can do for you, do not hesitate to ask."

"Will do."

Some of my fellow flyers had fancy champagne glasses in their hands. I was tempted to order one when the guy from the convenient store started walking my way.

My heart seemed to skip a beat as he stopped right in front of me. "It would seem we meet again." He flashed a charming smile. "What are the odds of that?"

"Slim to none," I whispered underneath my breath.

"Excuse me," he said as he shimmied his way to his seat by the window. Just those few moments of proximity had my body burning up. I tried to keep from blushing, but I could tell by the heat radiating from my face that I probably looked like a ripened tomato. "Seriously, what are the odds?" he asked once more as soon as he was settled into his seat. "Is it *Freaky Friday* or something?"

"It doesn't sound like you're very happy to see me."

"Oh no, not at all. I would rather sit beside you than

some of the uptights that usually ride first class." He tipped his head towards some older gentlemen wearing business suits. "I've had one guy on a conference call during the entirety of a six-hour flight. And, of course, that's when I forgot my headphones. I came this close to losing my mind."

"Jeez, I can only imagine," I said. "I promise I won't nag your ear off."

"Well, at least you have a nice voice."

The blush returned. "Oh, do I?"

"I think so," he smiled. "Do you sing at all?"

"Sing?" I scoffed. "Only in the shower."

"That's something." A grin flashed across his face. "I'd definitely pay to hear that."

"Careful," I warned. "You might be cute, but any more perverted comments and I might be forced to slow you."

"I didn't mean it like that." He held up both hands in a gesture of innocence.

Who was I kidding? Of course he didn't. A guy like this wouldn't waste his time with a girl like me. Still, there's no harm in dreaming...

I was about to say something when the captain's voice came on. "Hello!" He was overly chipper.

My flight buddy groaned. "I can already tell he's going to be the kind of pilot to crack jokes. I hope he's not the corny type."

"My name is Captain Phillips and I'll be taking you to Portland International. That's Portland, Maine. Those of you looking to get to Oregon, you better hitch up your wagons and head down the trail because you're on the wrong plane."

This time we both groaned.

"What did I tell you?"

"Do we have to suffer through this the entire flight?"

"I'm afraid so," he said. "I have some spare headphones if you need them."

"You carry around spares?"

"After what happened with conference call guy, yeah, I do."

"I might take you up on the offer."

We were forced to quiet down as the flight crew went through the safety drill. It was the same old spiel, but by law they were forced to show us how to inflate our lifejackets and whatnot.

When that was over, the plane became eerily quiet. I looked around and saw everyone tightening up their seatbelts. For some reason, I had failed to buckle myself in. I went to do so but the buckles wouldn't connect and lock together. "Um, excuse me." I tried to get the attention of one of the stewardesses, but she was busy helping someone else with their spoiled child.

"Here, let me," the unnamed surgeon reached over and took hold of the seatbelt. Since he had taken off his jacket, I was free to see his sculpted arms and the way his muscles moved underneath the skin. What a sight.

Click.

"Thanks," I breathed.

"Don't mention it."

"By the way, I never got your name."

"How rude of me," he said. "Name's Reed. And yours?"

"Winter."

"Winter," he repeated. The way he said my name had shivers running up and down my spine. "That's a nice name for a girl from Maine. Fitting."

"You think so? Our winters are so mild it's like they don't even exist," I said sarcastically.

He laughed. "Oh yeah, it's really easy to ignore ten feet of snow piled in your driveway."

"That's what I'm saying."

Wow, this guy was super easy to talk to. He just had a certain charisma that made him feel like a regular guy instead of this unapproachable hunk.

Suddenly, I felt the plane move. I gripped the arms of my seat. "I hate this part..." I whispered aloud.

To my surprise, Reed took hold of my hand and squeezed it against his. "Me too."

The plane picked up speed, forcing my heart to the back of my chest. Then came that weightless feeling of the plane taking off. It shook rather violently, catching a gust of air on its way up. If not for Reed's hand, I probably would have crapped my pants.

Finally, it leveled out and I was able to breathe again.

"That wasn't so bad."

"You're just saying that to make me feel better."

"Or to make myself feel better," he said.

The seatbelt light clicked off and everyone started to move. Reed was one of them. He grabbed the plastic bag that I had seen on his luggage earlier. Just as I had predicted, it was a brand-new laptop.

"One of the hazards of going to Florida for a medical conference is that you risk dropping your electronics into the water."

"What? You lost your laptop in the ocean or something?"

"Actually..." he struggled with the packaging as he spoke.

"How does that even happen?"

"Well, I was on a boat—"

"What kind of medical conference was this and how do I get an invite?"

He chuckled. "Well, you'd have to switch over to human medicine. I'm not sure if vets get the same perks."

"Such a rip-off." I pouted.

"Trust me, they aren't that great."

"You're riding first class," I pointed out.

"So are you," he countered.

"Only because they overbooked my original flight and this was my consolation prize."

"Nice." He booted up the computer. It was the newest model for the MacBook. If I had to guess, that thing was worth more than my monthly salary. "Anyway, where are you from?"

"Kittery."

"No kidding?"

"Why would I lie about that?"

"Well, it just so happens that I'm headed that way as well. I've worked in Boston for a while, but I was getting sick and tired of the city. I took a pay cut, but at least I get to come back to my home state. It'll be nice to enjoy that suburban peace and quiet."

"Do you have a place to stay?"

"Yeah, down by the Rafters."

"The Rafters?" I repeated. *That's where all the million-aires live,* I thought to myself. I mean, I know that doctors make good money, but even a heart surgeon doesn't crack a million.

"Yeah. An old friend of mine handles the real estate in that part of town. He was able to get me a pretty good deal."

I can only imagine what that deal was. I'll knock a couple of million off the ticket price.

"Well, I hope you like it. Kittery's kind of a sleepy little town."

"And that's exactly what I'm looking for."

"Any particular reason why you hate the city?"

"I don't hate it," he clarified. He seemed to be the kind of guy who was good at multitasking because somehow, he was having a full-blown conversation with me whilst setting up his computer with what seemed to be a million email accounts. "But there's this sort of atmosphere where everyone's out to get something. I felt like I couldn't breathe."

"Well, if you ever need some fresh air there's some pretty good hiking trails..." I was about to offer to take him but then I stopped myself. Sure, this guy was strikingly handsome and I couldn't deny the attraction I felt, but I wasn't going to let myself get wrapped up in yet another failed relationship. The last one had nearly ruined my chances of getting into veterinarian school. No. My dream comes before any dreamboat – that's the promise. I had to get through school first and *then* I might consider getting a boyfriend. Until then, I was riding solo.

--- End of Preview ---

***CONTINUE **reading FREE on Kindle Unlimited here!**

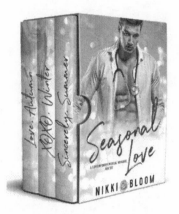

***or grab the standalone here (FREE w/ KU)!

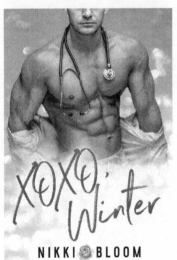

ABOUT THE AUTHOR

Thank you so much for reading!

I'm a contemporary romance writer who loves to write about billionaire bad boys! Join my mailing list here for freebies and promos regarding my upcoming releases!

Want the latest sneak peaks to upcoming cover reveals and free chapters? Join my private readers club here on Facebook and post!

A bit over a year ago, I took a leap of faith to pursue my dream of becoming a full-time writer. I love to get to know my readers personally so please connect with me for any feedback, questions, or even just to say hi!

info@nikkibloom.com

Nikki

ALSO BY NIKKI BLOOM (FREE W/ KU)

Seasonal Love Box Set

- Sincerely, Summer
- XOXO, Winter
- Love, Autumn

Protecting the Babysitter

His Fake Fiancé

The Billionaire Encounter

Freezing Touch (FREE on the next page)

Featured! 5/5 stars on Amazon.com

FREE BOOK OFFER!

Join my mailing list HERE to receive a FREE copy of "Freezing Touch"

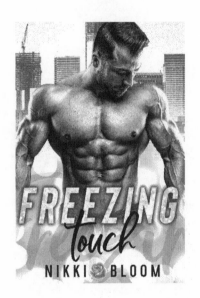